THE POWER OF POSITIVE PRANKING

BOOKS BY NAT AMOORE

Secrets of a Schoolyard Millionaire
The Power of Positive Pranking
The Right Way to Rock

We Run Tomorrow

THE POWER OF POSITIVE PRANKING

NAT AMOORE

PUFFIN BOOKS

PUFFIN BOOKS

UK | USA | Canada | Ireland | Australia

India | New Zealand | South Africa | China

Penguin
Random House
Australia

Penguin Random House Australia is part of the Penguin Random House group of companies whose addresses can be found at global.penguinrandomhouse.com.

First published by Puffin Books, an imprint of Penguin Random House Australia Pty Ltd, in 2020

Cover illustrations by James Lancett

Cover and text design by Tony Palmer © Penguin Random House Australia Pty Ltd

Printed and bound in Australia by Griffin Press, an accredited ISO AS/NZS 14001 Environmental Management Systems printer

NATIONAL LIBRARY OF AUSTRALIA

A catalogue record for this book is available from the National Library of Australia

ISBN 978 0 14 379638 1

Penguin Random House Australia uses papers that are natural and recyclable products, made from wood grown in sustainable forests. The logging and manufacture processes are expected to conform to the environmental regulations of the country of origin.

penguin.com.au

To all the kids who know they can make a difference . . .
. . . and especially for those who are still figuring it out.

GREEN PEAS MANIFESTO

GREEN PEAS RULE 1

THE FIRST RULE OF GREEN PEAS IS SHHHHHH!

I try to hide my nerves as our sports teacher, Ms Mezher, explains how Cross Country Day is going to work.

'And next Friday, Years Five and Six will meet in their assigned groups on the bottom oval at . . .'

I hold my breath and close my eyes. Here it comes . . .

Beep beep. Beep beep.

Ms Mezher stops for a moment and scans the school assembly. I keep my eyes fixed on the maths folder on my lap. That's only the first alarm clock. It's stuck to the bottom of a seat over near where Year Three sits. It's the little black clock with the red numbers. The first few I set to go off are the quieter ones: they'll build up slowly with one going off every minute until the grand finale under Mrs Keiren's butt.

Ms Mezher tries to ignore it, probably assuming some kid forgot to put their phone on silent, and continues with her weekly sports news.

'Um, at the beginning of lunch so that we can make sure . . .'

Beep beep. Beep beep.
Ding. Ding. Ding. Ding.

Some kids are starting to notice and look around. Teachers as well. I can't look too interested yet. The next one will go off under the seat just two rows in front of me – then I can pay attention. For now, I focus on my maths folder. My name is spelt out with stickers on the front and I pick at the 'W'. It was already partially coming off and I keep picking until it breaks in half so my name now reads 'Casey Vu' instead of 'Casey Wu'.

Ms Mezher is trying her best to stay on track.

'Er, make sure that everyone is checked off before we . . .'

Beep beep. Beep beep.
Ding. Ding. Ding. Ding.
Merp. Merp. Merp.

That's the one. The one two rows in front of me, under Amelie Berger's seat. She jumps into the air a little, looking around her. This alarm clock's louder than the first two. The kids near me start to giggle. Teachers stand up. I can pay attention now without looking suspicious.

Merp. Merp. Merp.

It's a pretty horrible sound – I can't imagine anyone wanting to wake up to that. Everyone's paying attention now. Ms Mezher has given up on her speech and is looking to the teachers on stage for help. A murmur spreads through the assembly. Heads turn left and right, confused. I join in, looking around. But I'm not confused. I know the next one will be in the Year Five section. And it'll be a good one.

I spent a lot of time planning this event. I tested all the alarm clocks and put them in order from quietest and most subtle to loudest and most obnoxious. Obnoxious is a great word. It sounds like some kind of disease and it has an 'X' in it. 'X' words always sound like they are attacking something.

I sat in assembly for weeks, secretly mapping out the chairs in my notebook and marking where everybody sits. Then I plotted where each alarm clock would go. I did test runs at home – syncing the clocks and setting them a minute apart. I laid them out in order on my bedroom floor, listened to them go off and adjusted everything for the right effect. All with Grandpa downstairs, happily watching his shows with closed captions on, no idea what I was up to just above him. It's one of the upsides to Grandpa being deaf – alarm clock testing doesn't bother him at all.

Zeke grins at me from the row in front, but I glare back at him. It's one of the Green Peas rules. 'No acknowledgement of other members during an event.' We moved it down on the list. Number 32, from memory. That doesn't make it any less important. But Zeke can't help himself. He's just so . . . Zeke!

I look at my watch. Here we go . . .

Beep beep. Beep beep.

Ding. Ding. Ding. Ding.

Merp. Merp. Merp.

Jingle bells, jingle bells, jingle all the way. Oh what fun it is to ride on a one-horse open sleigh. HEY!

I try my best not to smile as I think of the little Santa alarm clock gaffer-taped to the bottom of a Year Fiver's chair. I had to tape Santa around the stomach because his arms and legs move back and forth like he's making a snow angel when the alarm goes off.

Tess Heckleston catches my eye and gives me a wink. She's kept a pretty low profile since she got busted with that money thing a couple of months ago, but I should thank her for funding this event before she became as broke as the rest of us.

The assembly's in full chaos now. Kids are laughing and teachers are trying to calm everybody down – but it's not working at all. I knew it would go like this. That's why after the Santa clock, I set them all thirty seconds apart.

Beep beep. Beep beep.

Ding. Ding. Ding. Ding.

Merp. Merp. Merp.

Dashing through the snow in a one-horse open sleigh.

Buzz buzz buzz. Buzz buzz buzz.

Bring briiiiiiiing. Bring briiiiiiiing.

It's 8:40 am on WBS 107.2fm, and it's another beautiful day in Watterson.

BRAYNK! BRAYNK! BRAYNK! BRAYNK!

Driiiiing. Driiiiing.

Full pandemonium has set in now. I love the word 'pandemonium'. It sounds like what it is. I love words that do that.

And as I look around me at the mess our school assembly has become, there could not be a better word than 'pandemonium'.

Kids are standing on chairs or looking under them. Everyone can hear the noise, but hardly anyone knows where it's coming from. The teachers are shouting now, trying to get us all under control and find the source of the alarms. It's not going to work: I placed the clocks away from the aisle seats where the teachers are, and the kids are enjoying this way too much to help the teachers locate my clocks. This act of defiance is nothing if not well thought out.

I look at Mrs Keiren. Her face is turning slightly red, maybe even a little purple. Her hands clutch the armrests of the big wooden chair that sits on stage, fingernails digging into the wood. She looks like a kettle heating up. I know what's coming next, and my guess is it will be just enough to make her boil over.

I can see the back of Cookie's head from where I'm sitting. She doesn't turn around. She can follow the Green Peas rules way better than Zeke, but the tension in the back of her neck tells me she can't wait for the next bit either.

I look at my watch. 8:44 am. Seconds to go.

Beep beep. Beep beep.

Ding. Ding. Ding. Ding.

Merp. Merp. Merp.

Over the hills we go, laughing all the way. HO HO HO!

Buzz buzz buzz. Buzz buzz buzz.

Bring briiiiiiiing. Bring briiiiiiiing.

Reaching twenty-four today with clear skies and no chance of –

BRAYNK! BRAYNK! BRAYNK! BRAYNK!

Driiiiing. Driiiiing.

And three, two, one . . .

BWAK BWAK BAGAAAAARK!

The chicken alarm clock goes off under Mrs Keiren's butt . . . and the kettle boils over. SHE . . . IS . . . FUMING! I can almost see the steam coming out of her ears. The entire school stops and turns to face the principal.

BWAK BWAK BAGAAAAARK!

Mrs Keiren leaps up like she's just laid an egg, and the school erupts into laughter. She reaches under her chair and rips off a chicken alarm clock covered in gaffer tape. The plastic chicken in her hand flaps its wings.

BWAK BWAK BAGAAAAARK!

With that, timed as perfectly as I'd hoped, a banner drops from the ceiling of the school hall.

WAKE UP! DINOSAURS THOUGHT THEY HAD TIME TOO. SAVE OUR PLANET NOW.

I smile proudly. It's fine to do that now; my grin will be lost in the craziness around me. None of the teachers suspect that the quiet kid with the maths folder is behind the elaborate protests. Or, as Mrs Keiren is calling them, 'pranks'.

But I, Casey Wu, am not just a prankster. I am an activist. I may be only eleven years old, but I have a lot to say, and I will be heard. No matter how loud I have to be.

Sometimes, you need to take action to make a difference. Everyone can stand up in their own way. Every activist has their own superpower.

And mine is pranking.

I slide one of Mum's cards out of my folder. It seemed appropriate to bring this one with me today.

Trixie Wu's Thoughts On . . .

MAKING A DIFFERENCE

You only get one life, Casey-baby. Make it count. Make a difference, whatever you want that to be - big or small, to one person or to the whole world. Be the change you want to see. Find your strength and use it.

xMum

GREEN PEAS RULE 2

It's not about the glory, it's about the message.

I get a few low fives as I make my way back to class. Green Peas isn't a total secret at Watterson Primary, but kids here don't dob on each other. I mean, if someone is hurting another kid or bullying them or something, there's no code – you absolutely go down for something like that. But when it comes to 'kids' business', we sort of look out for each other.

I take my usual seat in Mr Deery's class between Zeke and Cookie. Cookie gives me a slight nod – she's so cool and super-spy-like. Zeke's breaking the rules as usual. He's grinning ear to ear and gives me a double thumbs-up. I just ignore him. It's the approach I often take with Zeke.

Mr Deery stumbles in looking pretty frazzled. It took a long time for the teachers to get everyone under control, out of assembly and back to their classes. Mr Deery used to teach Year Five, but everything got reshuffled when Mr Bijac went on paternity leave. It was a good trade. Mr Bijac smelled like feet. But not just his feet smelled like feet. His suit smelled like used socks. His aftershave smelled like old leather. And his breath . . . well, you know the black stuff that builds up under the corners of your toenails? Mr Bijac's breath smelled like he ate that for breakfast. BLAH!

So Mr Deery and his peppermint smell is a definite upgrade.

'Okay, kids, we're going to try to move on from this morning's little, um, disruption,' Mr Deery says, rearranging the papers on his desk for the third time.

'Disruption'. I like that. It's a much better word than 'prank'.

Well done, Mr Deery, that's exactly what we're trying to do – disrupt the way the world is going. I scribble the word 'disruption' in my workbook.

Mr Deery finally finds the book he's looking for and waves it at the class. 'Can we all get our workbooks out, turn to page thirty-four, and we'll put this morning behind us and get onto some learning?'

A crackle in the speaker on the ceiling tells me Mrs Keiren has other ideas.

'Students!' Mrs Keiren's voice screeches through the speaker. It's so loud and distorted that it sounds like she has the microphone shoved halfway down her throat. 'Today's display of anarchy will not be tolerated.'

I jot down the word 'anarchy' on the corner of my workbook. I like the sound of that one too. Not the sound of it squawking through the speakers at me care of Mrs Keiren, of course, but the sound of it as I roll it around in my head. I make a note to look it up later.

'These pranks are no laughing matter, and the students behind them will be found, mark my word. You may think you're making some kind of statement, but this is **NOT** the way to make yourself heard.'

I disagree. No one listens to you when you're a kid, even when you have something really important to say. We tried to ask the supermarket at Watto Mall to stop using single-use plastic bags, but we couldn't even speak to anyone higher up than the half-asleep seventeen-year-old who ran the assistance counter. Which, by the way, should definitely be renamed. The Green Peas events are my way – our way – of yelling so loud they can't ignore us.

The screeching continues. 'I expect *anyone* who knows *anything* about this matter to report to my office and give themselves, or the offending students, up immediately!'

The speaker crackles once more and falls silent. Mr Deery sighs.

'Does anyone want to come forward?' Mr Deery asks, looking around the classroom. The kids all look at each other. Zeke, Cookie and I join in. Nobody raises their hand. I love my school.

'Very well, then. Let's put the matter behind us and move on with our comprehension exercises.'

As Mr Deery opens up his exercise book, Mac Cooper's hand shoots up. I hold my breath for a second. I don't know if Mac knows about us. He's a bit of a muso at school, plays guitar in a band and has that special ability to look blasé about pretty much everything. 'Blasé' basically means 'whatevs', but it sounds way more sophisticated, don't you think? It's one of my new favourite words. Anyway, Mac seems like a cool kid. I don't think he'd dob us in. But you never know.

Mr Deery looks up. 'Yes, Mac?'

'Maybe instead of just ignoring the prank or trying to bust the kids who did it, we should talk about why it happened.' Mac flicks his hair away from his eyes and shrugs.

Maybe Mac's not just a cool muso type after all. I'm impressed. I take back my label of blasé and make note to find a more appropriate adjective for Mac. I turn to Mr Deery, super keen to hear his answer.

'Okay,' he says, closing the book in front of him. 'What do you want to talk about?'

'Not sure,' says Mac. 'But it's not just another prank, right? I mean whoever's doing it is trying to get our attention. To – you know – think about our planet and how we're wrecking it. I mean it's kinda scary for us kids. With climate change and everything, are we even gonna have a planet to live on?'

My belly's doing flip flops. This is EXACTLY what I wanted. Mr Bijac would have shut this conversation down by now, but Mr Deery is different.

He nods. 'You're right, Mac. I agree: it's scary. Does anyone else worry about this sort of thing?' Every hand shoots up, including my own.

'All right then,' he says. 'Let's talk about it. Comprehension can wait until after lunch.'

We all close our books.

Mr Deery rubs his forehead. 'Now, it's a pretty big subject. Does anyone have anywhere in particular they want to start?'

Every hand in the class shoots up again.

Mr Deery points to Isla. 'Let's start with you, Isla.'

She drops her hand. 'I think it's really hard to know what we should do about it. I mean, I don't really like being in big crowds at protests, or public speaking, but I want to help too.'

Mr Deery nods. 'I think the first thing we should talk about is how you can find your own way to take a stance for what you believe in. Some people do it through science or politics, and others through protests or writing. Why don't we talk about some of the ways you can help. Any ideas?'

Hands go up again.

I can't hide my grin this time. See! I knew kids have a lot to say.

I quickly scribble down the word 'apathetic' in my folder as I race to the garden shed. I just needed to check a few words with Mr Deery after class, so Zeke and Cookie went ahead without me.

My handwriting's terrible because it's super hard to run and write at the same time, but I don't want to forget this word. Mr Deery said it at the very end of class when we were talking about why grown-ups don't do more about what's happening to our planet. I want to make sure I don't forget it.

I've always loved new words. I want to have a really big vocabulary so that I can explain exactly what I'm thinking and how I'm feeling. Writing's my favourite subject at school for sure. Maybe I'll be a writer when I grow up. But probably an activist. I wonder if you can be both. Zeke's stepdad has two jobs, so why not?

Realising I've slowed to a walk, I run the rest of the way to the garden shed.

I do the secret knock and Zeke lets me in. 'Sorry I'm late.'

'No worries,' he says. 'Mr Deery said a bunch of new words that I figured you'd want to add to the list.'

Sometimes I think Zeke knows me too well.

I take a seat next to Cookie and pass her the Green Peas folder. Her t-shirt today says, 'TREES ARE PEOPLE TOO', and there's a cartoon of a girl hugging a tree.

'One of yours?' I ask.

Cookie nods. 'Dad and Aaron got me a bunch of new t-shirt transfer paper for my birthday. This was the tester.'

'I love it.' Cookie always makes the best shirts.

I turn to Zeke. 'Did you collect the cameras?' He's always in charge of making sure our events are recorded.

He pats his satchel. I know – what eleven-year-old has a satchel? It's so antiquated. It's so . . . Zeke!

'Roger!' he says, giving me a salute.

'Just say *yes*, Zeke.'

'Roger that,' he says again.

I give up.

The garden shed gives a metallic grumble as it leans in the wind. This is where we meet every second lunchtime – unless there's an event coming up, and then the meetings are more often. No . . . more frequent. I heard that word on the news last night. 'More frequent bushfires are an effect of global climate change.' I like words with a 'Q' in the middle. They sound fancy. No . . . they sound eloquent.

Zeke sits up straight, like he's reporting for duty. 'I snuck the cameras back out of the hall without anyone suspecting a thing,' he says proudly. 'I even came back to class with a small piece of toilet paper stuck to my foot to convince everybody that I'd actually gone to the bathroom. It was very ninja-like.'

I look at Zeke from under my eyebrows. 'You're *not* a ninja, Zeke.'

'Well, wouldn't it be very ninja-like for someone to be a ninja and for their best friend-slash-neighbour to not even know they were a ninja?' Zeke tilts his head to the side. 'Hmm? Think about it.'

I turn to Cookie. She's much easier to deal with.

'Great banner today, Cookie. I especially enjoyed the little T-Rex you did munching on the "T".'

Cookie opens our Green Peas folder up in her lap. 'Actually, it was a Diplodocus. They're vegetarian so they only eat . . . "T"s!'

Zeke slaps his leg. 'Ha! I get it. "T"s! Trees! And it's a layered message because they're vegetarian. Get it, Casey?'

I glare at him. 'Yes, Zeke, thank you. I get it.'

'So good, Cookie,' he says, shaking his head. 'So, so good.'

Cookie laughs. 'Thanks, Zeke. I appreciate your appreciation.'

'All right,' I say, tapping my finger on the folder. 'Can we get back to it? What's next on the agenda?'

Cookie thumbs through the official Green Peas folder and stops on today's page. 'You wanted to do Plastic Attack next weekend.'

I rub my chin dramatically, deep in contemplation. 'Contemplation' is even deeper thinking than thought. Super deep. 'No, I don't think we'll be ready for next weekend. The alarm clock prank took a bit more preparation than I expected and it's put us behind schedule.'

Zeke grins at me. 'But it was awesome.'

I let a small smile creep onto my lips. 'Yes, Zeke. It was awesome.' I know Rule 2 says, 'It's not about the glory, it's about the message', but seeing Mrs Keiren jump into the air at that chicken noise – that was the kind of glory that's hard not to enjoy.

Cookie gets us back on our agenda. 'How does Plastic Attack work? Is it something I can help fast track?'

I refocus. 'That's the one where everyone has to bring containers and stuff to the supermarket to do their shopping, and before they leave they unpack everything packaged in single-use wrapping and leave the plastic at the front of the store. I saw a video of it in the Netherlands. There was a huge pile of plastic showing the supermarkets how much waste they cause. We should do it at Watto Mall, seeing as we didn't have much luck with the plastic bag thing.'

Cookie takes notes. 'Well, I can definitely do signs and stuff, but yeah, I reckon we need a bit more time to really spread the word. How about I put it down for next month?'

'Okay,' I agree. 'But it would be good to do something else before then.'

Zeke holds his finger in the air like a cartoon character having an idea. 'How about we put whoopee cushions on all the teachers' chairs that say, "You stink . . . but garbage stinks more! RECYCLE!"'

I grab his finger and drag it down. 'What did we discuss about the whoopee cushions? We're trying to go for a more sophisticated image, remember?'

Zeke nods. 'Yeah, sorry, it's just sometimes my brain has a mind of its own.'

Cookie laughs. 'How can your brain have a . . .' she starts, but stops when I give her 'the look'.

I point to the folder again. 'Let's move on, shall we?'

The school garden shed is not that bad this time of year. In summer it's so hot that after fifteen minutes we start to steam like dim sum. We've been meeting here for almost a year now. It's been that long since I started Green Peas, our covert environmental activism group. I got the idea from Mum.

Trixie Wu's Thoughts On . . .

YOUR TRIBE

It's important to find your tribe, Casey. That doesn't necessarily mean people *like* you, it means people who complement you. Some people educate. Some people learn. Some lead. Some follow. Some shout. Some whisper. Your tribe should be a beautiful mix of it all. Find the friends that make you a better person and then hold on tight.

xMum

You can't be a group on your own. Not even a covert group. So I hunted for my tribe. The Green Peas' first member (other than me) was Zeke, mostly because he was the only other kid I really knew. People always ask me if Zeke is my best friend. Truth is, my grandpa's my best friend, but I would never admit that out loud. Zeke's definitely my longest friend, though.

Cookie joined the group because I saw her wearing a t-shirt that said, 'THERE'S NO PLANET B'. I asked her where she bought it and she told me she'd made it. She buys all her clothes at Vinnies and then creates designs to transfer onto them. I pretty much thought that was the coolest thing ever, and so, of course, I asked her to join the group. She even designed Green Peas t-shirts for us, which made us so much more legitimate. Or, as they say on any B-grade TV reality show – totes legit!

And so now this is us, the Green Peas: Casey Wu, Zeke McKillop and Cookie Munsta. Cookie's real name is Chloe, but she HATES it when people call her that. She made the teacher change the roll call on her FIRST DAY at school! I don't think I spoke a single word on my first day of school.

But I digress (a great word which means to go off on a total tangent . . . like I'm doing again now). Green Peas are defenders of the planet, creators of anarchy, kids demanding to be heard (while staying completely anonymous and out of detention). We all bring something different to the group. Cookie's super creative and arty (and definitely the coolest of us). Zeke is the tech-guy (and definitely NOT a ninja, no matter what he says). And me? I guess I'm the organiser. The planner. Maybe the ideas person? I'm still working it out. I'll get back to you.

The garden shed groans in the wind again and leans at an awkward angle. Zeke points to the giant pile of plastic water bottles that's threatening to topple down on his head. 'Have you decided what you want to do with those yet?'

I shake my head. 'Not yet, but keep collecting them. Once we have enough, we'll do something to make the canteen stop selling them. I mean seriously, how hard is it to bring a drink bottle and use the fountain?'

'And cheaper,' says Cookie.

A bottle rolls from the top and the pile sways enough to suggest an avalanche might be coming. 'Maybe we could borrow a box from the art room to put them all in,' I suggest.

'Roger that!' says Zeke.

I can't handle him anymore. 'All right, let's wrap it up.'

'There *was* one more thing,' says Zeke.

'What?'

'Our secret handshake. I really think we need one.'

I shake my head at him. 'I really think we don't.'

Zeke slides his satchel over his shoulder as he stands up. 'Okie dokie. Maybe at the next meeting then.' He salutes me and walks out of the garden shed.

Cookie follows him, but stops at the door and turns to me. 'You know you could try to be a bit nicer to him,' she says.

I sigh. 'I don't mean to be rude. But he's just so . . .'

'Zeke?' Cookie smirks.

'Exactly!' I follow Cookie out and watch Zeke head straight for the computer room.

See, SO Zeke!

GREEN PEAS RULE 3

PRANKS MUST *ALWAYS* BE FOR THE GREATER GOOD.

At the end of the day, as I walk out of school, I see Zeke leaning against the fence reading some tech magazine.

I give him a wave. 'Hey!'

Zeke closes his mag. 'Wanna walk home together?'

I fiddle with the strap on my school bag. 'Nah, I can't.'

'Going via Brennan Park?' he asks.

I nod.

'Cool,' says Zeke, tossing the magazine in his bag. 'I'll take Yatama Road, then. See ya!'

I watch him head off, his satchel jingling with key rings. 'Hey, Zeke, wait! You can walk home with me if you want?'

He stops and turns to look over his shoulder. 'Nah, I get it, Casey. We all need some solo time.'

I kick at the dirt a little. 'I don't want to be mean.'

'You're not mean. You're real. I'll see you at home. Say hi to your mum for me.' With that, his satchel jingles away down the road.

Zeke may not be a ninja, but he's pretty cool. I chuck my bag over my shoulder and head for Brennan Park.

Cutting through the top entrance of the park, I head straight for Mum's bench. I take off my bag and sit down. The familiar strips of wood push into my back and I curl my neck over the bend at the top, staring up through the branches of the big grey ironbark tree that looms over the seat. The leaves move in the breeze, letting bits of sunlight sneak through before they shift and the light disappears again. I close my eyes and listen to the rustling. Somewhere further down the park, a man is yelling at his dog and the dog barks an answer. There's a soft hum of cars passing on the far side.

It's so tranquil. Love those 'Q' words.

I open my eyes and turn sideways on the seat, rubbing my fingers over the worn brass plaque on the wood.

IN LOVING MEMORY OF TRIXIE WU.

HER FAVOURITE PLACE, HER FAVOURITE TREE,

OUR FAVOURITE PERSON.

I take another one of Mum's cards out of my wallet. Most of them are in the little recipe card box at home, but this one stays with me so I can always read it here. It's all worn around the edges, and even has a bit of soy sauce on it from a sushi lunch a few months ago.

Trixie Wu's Thoughts On . . .

THE BIG GREY IRONBARK

I love this tree, Casey. I've spent hours and hours sitting under it with your father, with you, alone. It's a great place to think. If you need some time to think, come sit under this tree. I swear life just seems better under it.

xMum

She's right. I love this tree too.

This is one of the first cards Mum wrote especially for me. Dad got them printed for her as an anniversary present before I was born. A leafy vine design decorates the border on each one, and they all have 'TRIXIE WU'S THOUGHTS ON . . .' printed at the top. Dad says she had so many thoughts in her head that she should have somewhere special to write them all down.

So she did.

She started writing on the cards and placing them in a recipe card box. First it was one, and then two and then ten. They started off as just general thoughts about all kinds of things, whatever was on her mind. But later on, when she got sick and I was just a baby, she started writing them to me. I have all of them now. And I read them every day. They make me feel closer to her.

As I tuck the card back into my wallet, I hear the strumming of a guitar. Over at the Lego house, Kooky Kathy is playing a song I don't recognise. The bright plastic structure stands in the middle of the park like a funky installation art piece. The kids of Watterson Primary have done some pretty cool things in their time, but building Kathy's Lego house probably tops the list. Kathy gives me a wave and I wave back. Like most of the kids in Watterson, I love Kathy. She's the nucleus of our town – that means the centre, most important part. Ok, maybe she's the second most important part – her pet ferret Mr Piddles is my favourite. I still have a rice cracker left over from my lunch, so I head over to feed Mr Piddles.

'Hi Kathy.'

She doesn't stop playing but answers in tune. 'Well, hello there, young Casey, young Casey Wu. As always a delight to encounter you-uuuu!'

It always gets interesting when Kathy makes up her own lyrics.

'Is it okay if I feed Mr Piddles?' I ask. The brown and white ferret is perched on Kathy's shoulder, staring at me hopefully with his shiny black eyes.

'There's nothing Mr Piddles likes more, than food being shoved in his jaaaaaw!'

I smile politely at the singing and go ahead and hold the cracker out to Mr Piddles. He takes a few sniffs and then a nibble.

'Hold your arm out,' says Kathy. I do as I'm told and she does the same, our fingertips touching. Mr Piddles scurries from Kathy's shoulder, running down her arm and onto mine, zooming around the back of my neck to lie across my shoulders. His claws tickle my skin through my school uniform as I feed him the rest of the cracker.

Kathy strums thoughtfully on her guitar. 'Saying hi to your mum?'

'Yup,' I say. 'That's her bench.'

'I know,' Kathy says. 'I remember when her and all those uni kids chained themselves to that ironbark.'

'Yeah, I have that photo at home.' I laugh. 'She seriously loved that tree. Weird, huh?'

Kathy shrugs. 'I dunno. You love what you love. I love Mr Piddles and some people think that's weird.'

I scratch the top of Mr Piddles' head. 'That's not weird at all. Mr Piddles is awesome.'

Kathy stands next to me and the ferret leaps from my shoulder to hers. 'I wholeheartedly agree,' she says.

'Okay, see you, Kathy. Bye, Mr Piddles.'

As I head for home I hear Kathy's voice singing to her best friend. 'And here's to you, Mr Piddles, Kathy loves you more than you could know. Woah, woah, woah.'

Stopping in front of our brown brick apartment block, I check the mailbox, but it all looks pretty boring. Mostly bills and stuff, and some pamphlet about voting for Mayor Lupphol again at the next election. I don't know why she wastes her money on advertising – nobody has run against her in years. I mean, a few have tried, but they always drop out before the election for one reason or another, leading to her consistent landslide victory. It's a waste of trees, printing this garbage. I almost put the flyer straight in the recycling bin, but decide I should probably keep it in case Grandpa wants to read it. I'm pretty sure Dad won't care.

'Hey!'

I spin around, nearly jumping out of my skin, to see Zeke looming behind me.

'Don't sneak up on me like that, Zeke!'

'I can't help it, sorry. It's a ninja thing.'

'You're NOT a ninja, Zeke. You're almost two metres tall with bright red hair. You couldn't be invisible if you tried,' I say, giving him a shove.

'Says the one who didn't hear me sneak up on her,' Zeke answers, a triumphant grin plastered across his freckled face. He nods slowly. 'Much like a ninja, you might say.'

‘What do you want, Zeke?’ I’m not having the ninja argument again.

He holds a USB up in front of my face.

‘You can’t have edited it already,’ I say, snatching the stick off him.

‘Yup,’ he says. ‘Did some at lunch after the meeting and finished it off while you were in the park.’

I try not to look too impressed. ‘You need to get out more.’

‘I do. At night. Like all good ninjas.’

I shake my head at him, but laugh. ‘All right, ninja boy, I’m going in. You want to come over for dinner tonight? Dad’s working, so it’s just me and Grandpa.’

‘Maybe. I’ll see what’s going on at home.’

‘Okay. Bye.’

Zeke slips around the fence as I head into our building. Pulling out my keys, I unlock the door to our apartment. As I walk in, I press the doorbell so the red light in the kitchen flashes and Grandpa knows I’m home. Kicking off my shoes, I dump my bag as he comes to the end of the hall.

‘Casey-poo!’ he yells, with a grin.

'Hi, Ah Gong!' Sliding down the corridor in my socks, I give him a big hug, then pull back so he can see my lips. 'Has Dad left yet?'

He shakes his head. 'Not yet, he's just getting ready. Want something to eat?'

I nod and follow Grandpa inside. Taking a seat on the kitchen stool, I watch as he moves around the kitchen. Because Grandpa is deaf, I have to wait until he's looking at me before I can talk to him, so he can read my lips. Some people think all deaf people can lip-read but that's totally not true. It's actually super hard to do, but Grandpa's awesome at it.

He says it's because he was a super-spy when he lived in Singapore. But he left Singapore when he was a teenager and went deaf when he was in his twenties, so I've done the maths and I'm pretty sure I don't believe him, but with Grandpa you just never know.

As he gets my snack ready, he shuffles around the kitchen in his slippers. He's pretty small, my grandpa, with just a little bit of hair left around the sides of his head and a whole lot of bald on the top. He's missing a couple of teeth and his ears seem a bit too big for his head. He says he doesn't understand why his ears keep growing at his age, especially when they don't even work, but I think Grandpa is perfect. He reminds me a bit of Yoda from *Star Wars*. And it's not just the way he looks. He's full of hard-to-follow grandpa wisdom too.

He turns and narrows his eyes at me. 'What's that look?'

'Nothing,' I say, picturing him in a brown robe with his face painted green. I think I'm going to make him go as Yoda for Halloween this year. 'Just admiring your funny-shaped head.'

He closes his hand in front of his mouth, which is sign language for 'shut up'. Grandpa doesn't know a lot of sign language, even though he and I did a course last year. Zeke came too, because he thought it would add to his ninja-repertoire and he'd already taught himself Morse code. Grandpa says it's one of his biggest regrets, not learning sign language when he started going deaf. He says there's a whole wonderful Deaf culture out there that he sort of missed out on.

I thought the sign language classes were fun. We all learnt the sign alphabet and some basic sentences, and Grandpa picked up a few rude words too. Sometimes we use it to have secret conversations that Dad can't follow. This drives Dad crazy, of course, but he said he was too busy to do the classes with us, so that's on him.

'I bought some of these today,' Grandpa says, sliding a packet of Oreos towards me on the counter. 'And this is good for your bones.' A glass of milk is plopped down in front of me.

Yes! I love Oreos, and Dad never buys them for me. I grab the first one from the pack and shovel the whole thing into my mouth.

Blergh! The Oreo comes flying out again as quickly as it went in, spraying chocolate biscuit all over Grandpa. He laughs hysterically.

'AH GONG!' I yell, spitting the toothpaste-covered chocolate lumps out of my mouth.

Grandpa grabs his stomach and points a wrinkly finger at me. 'Got you! Got you!' He's laughing so hard he can barely get the words out. 'I scraped the cream out and filled it with toothpaste. HA! You should see your face!'

I take a mouthful of milk to wash out the toothpaste taste. I stop for a second, scared that maybe it's not milk at all, but it tastes normal so I swish it around my mouth.

I'm annoyed at myself for not seeing this one coming. Grandpa and I have been pranking each other since I can remember. We're so experienced that these days it's hard to catch each other out, but he was lucky this time – he caught me at a weak (and hungry) moment. I was distracted by the lure of the Oreo. It also means that I have to plan my next attack on him in retaliation.

The pranking started when I was a baby. He gave me a piece of lemon to suck just so he could take a photo of me with a face like a cat's bum, and it's been back and forth ever since. I put Glad Wrap over his toilet seat. He sewed up the arm holes of my favourite t-shirts. I changed his mobile phone's language to Turkish. He replaced my shampoo with hair gel. I filled his slippers with shaving cream. You get the idea.

'It's okay,' Grandpa says, finally getting his laughter under control. 'I only did the first one.'

He pushes the rest of the packet towards me. I hesitate, unsure. He jiggles the biscuits at me. 'C'mon on, Casey-poo. You know I never lie. Prank, but not lie.'

I snatch an Oreo and nibble on it. Tastes normal. Tastes good. I stuff the whole thing in my mouth and grab another.

Grandpa leans on the kitchen bench. 'How was school?'

I shrug. 'Fine, I guess.' I realise my mouth's full, which makes it really hard for Grandpa to understand what I'm saying. I wash the Oreo down with a glass of milk and try again. 'It was fine, Ah Gong. Learnt a lot, didn't get in trouble.'

Grandpa gives a little snort. 'Well, that's no fun, is it?' He goes back to stirring something on the stove that I think might be laksa. Something I *hope* might be laksa.

I hear Dad's footsteps coming down the stairs and spin around for my hug.

'Well, hello there, my favourite girl,' Dad says as he gives me a big squeeze. His hearing aid whistles against my cheek. It always does that when something presses against his ear.

Both my dad and my grandpa have a thing called otosclerosis. Cool word, huh? It sounds like a name of a dinosaur (which Grandpa pretty much is), but it's actually a condition where a bone grows in your ear, which stops things from vibrating properly inside, which stops you from hearing properly. It's hereditary, so that means it gets passed down in your family.

Grandpa's mum had it too. Back then (because this was almost *actual* dinosaur time), they thought she was going deaf because of her teeth, so they pulled them all out! I mean seriously, what a ridiculous way to try to fix hearing loss – by yanking out someone's teeth! But this was back around the same time they thought it was a brilliant idea to release cane toads into Australia, so who knows what they were thinking?

The whistling is so loud that I gently push Dad away from my cheek. He laughs and adjusts his hearing aid.

'Sorry, hon. How was school?'

Grandpa answers for me. 'She didn't do anything interesting. Just sat around and learnt stuff.

Boring!' He winks at me and flashes a grin with plenty of missing teeth. Don't worry, his just fell out on their own.

'Well, that sounds perfect to me,' Dad says, tucking his security guard shirt into his navy pants. 'I'm happy to be the parent of a boring kid. Unlike those pranksters taking over the school, right, Casey?'

I freeze for a second. How does he know about . . .

'What?' yells Grandpa. 'What's that? Another prank.' He turns to me. 'Is that what he said? He was looking at his belt buckle.'

Dad looks up at Grandpa. 'Sorry, Dad. Yes, all the parents got an email from the school today. Another prank, this time at assembly.'

Grandpa lights up and turns to me. 'So not such a boring day at school after all?' He gives me a knowing smile. 'Any idea who the culprits are?'

I glare back at him. Grandpa knows about Green Peas, but he plays ignorant. It's a sort of unspoken agreement. We both know if Dad found out, I'd be dead meat, so Grandpa doesn't ask, and I don't tell.

This way he also has plausible deniability, which means if Green Peas ever get busted, only *I* will get grounded.

He's also been read the rules, so he knows not to talk about Green Peas in front of Dad. But he just loves to antagonise me. 'No, Ah Gong. We all have *no* idea who it is.'

Grandpa nods. 'Ah, remaining undetected. They must come from a long line of super-spies.'

I shoot a look at Dad but he's focused on attaching his security pass. Grandpa continues.

'Will they put it on the YouTelly like the others?'

'It's *YouTube*, Ah Gong. And yeah, probably.'

Grandpa rubs his hands together like a comic book villain. 'Yaaaaassss!'

Dad shakes his head. 'You shouldn't encourage this kind of delinquency.' He points at the Oreos. 'And you shouldn't buy that junk either.'

'Oh pooey,' Grandpa replies. 'Junk food and good pranks make the world go round. You need to lighten up a little. You're as stuffy as that uniform.'

I think Dad looks good in his uniform. He's a night security guard at Watto Mall, which sounds more exciting than it is. He tells me he mostly just sits by himself in a room with lots of screens listening to podcasts. Dad recently got Bluetooth hearing aids that connect directly to his iPhone so podcasts are his new favourite thing. I don't think security-guarding is his dream job, but he says he likes being alone. Not having to talk to anyone. Lots of time to think. I wonder what he thinks about. Mum?

'You can call me stuffy all you want,' says Dad. 'But as far as I'm concerned, those kids should spend less time fooling around and more time learning.'

'I think they're trying to make a difference, Dad,' I say quietly.

He does up the top button on his shirt. 'Well, that's not the way to go about it.'

'And what would you know,' says Grandpa. 'When's the last time you did something for the greater good?'

Dad grinds his teeth a little. I know he and Grandpa love each other, but they really know how to get on each other's nerves.

Dad takes a deep breath. 'How about every night when I leave home to go and make the money that keeps this roof over our heads?' He turns his head and mumbles under his breath. 'Including yours?'

I hate it when Dad does that. He, more than anyone, knows how unfair it is to talk about Grandpa without looking at him. Dad and Grandpa both had surgery for their otosclerosis. Dad's went well – he can hear okay with his hearing aids. Grandpa's went badly and he lost his hearing completely. You would think this would give them something to bond over, but somehow they still seem to have zero patience with each other. I can feel a fight brewing and decide changing the subject is the best move.

'Are you leaving now, Dad?' I ask. 'Or do you have time for dinner with us?'

Dad looks at his watch. 'I think I'd better take it to go, sorry. Alil wants to knock off early today.'

'Okay, I'll get it ready for you.'

'Thanks, hon.' He kisses my cheek and goes into the hallway to put his boots on. I join

Grandpa, who has returned to stirring the pot. A quick peek inside tells me it's the laksa I was hoping for. I put my hand on Grandpa's arm and wait for him to face me. 'Dad's going to take his with him, okay?'

Grandpa nods. I grab a container and together we pack Dad's dinner. 'How about a game of Scrabble after the laksa?' I ask.

'You bet,' says Grandpa. 'And we can polish off the rest of the Oreos while we're at it.'

'Oh yeah, Dad would love that!'

Grandpa snaps the lid on Dad's dinner. 'Well, when your dad's at work, we live by Ah Gong rules. Plus,' he lowers his voice, 'I want to hear all about the little prank at school today.'

I take the container. 'Oh, Ah Gong, there was *nothing* little about it.'

GREEN PEAS RULE 4

Stay off the grid.

After Dad leaves for work, we eat dinner and Grandpa's now annihilating me in a game of Scrabble. Annihilating is like beating, but it hurts your ego way worse.

'Board games keep your brain alive, Casey-poo,' he says. 'Computers rot brain cells.' I don't think that's true at all, but I don't mind playing Scrabble with Grandpa.

He lays his tiles down on the board to spell 'FLATULENCE'.

'What's that mean?' I ask.

He sniggers. 'It's a fancy word for fart!'

'Ah Gong! You're supposed to be the grown-up here. Little immature, maybe?'

'What? I'm not *that* short, Casey. Wait till you get old, you'll shrink too.'

'What?' I say, confused. 'What are you talking about?'

'Didn't you just call me "miniature"?'

I burst out laughing. '*Immature*, Ah Gong!' I get my laughter under control so I can mouth the word more clearly to him. 'Immature.'

Grandpa laughs too. 'Oh, well *that* I am.' He counts up his letters. 'But, with a double word score, I may be immature but I'm also leading by twenty-four points! If I keep playing like this, I'll whip those oldies tomorrow.'

'Those oldies are your friends,' I say.

'Frenemies!' he corrects me. 'On Tuesdays, they're my competition. And I plan on maintaining my winning streak.'

I stare at the impossible number of consonants that are sitting on my Scrabble rack. I'm trying to make a decent word out of the four 'R's that stare back at me, but it's not easy. The best I can come up with is 'RAT', and I know better than to try a three-letter word when playing with Grandpa. I'd never hear the end of it.

'I can't find any good words,' I complain.

'Stop talking and concentrate,' says Grandpa. 'Let the letters speak to you. You know "listen" is an anagram of "silent".'

I hate it when Grandpa gets all Scrabble-guru on me. He's awesome at anagrams, but I don't think *that* particular trait is hereditary. I stare at my letters, waiting for them to speak to me, but all they say is 'RRRR'. I think I'll just let him win.

After being totally whipped at Scrabble, I've gone back to my room. Grandpa's downstairs watching *Mr Bean*, and me and my belly full of laksa are lying on my bed, still trying to digest. I had two bowls, which is way too much, but Grandpa makes the best laksa ever. He says he got the recipe from Mr Lee Kuan Yew's – that's Singapore's first prime minister – personal chef. I'm pretty sure that's not true. But, you know, it's Grandpa, so it could be. Apparently he secretly smuggled the recipe over from Singapore, written in Hokkien so no one in Australia could read it. Considering there are three families on our street alone who speak Hokkien, I think he might be exaggerating its secrecy. It *is* delicious, though, I'll give him that.

We had to do a family history thing at school last year, but when Grandpa tried to help, it got so convoluted. I think even *he's* forgotten where he lived and when. From what I can work out, Grandpa moved from Singapore to Australia when he was a teenager, then went back and forth a bit during his life. Dad was born in Singapore, but lived most of his life in Australia. Dad met Mum at uni, got married and had me. Grandpa was back in Singapore, then, but when Mum died he moved over to live with us permanently. Confusing, huh?

As the laksa gurgles in my belly, my eyes rest on the collage of photos of Mum on my bedroom wall. I don't think I have any real memories of her. I try really hard, but I think I was just too young. I wish I had some. Just one even. What I do have is lots of photos.

There's one of Mum giving me a bath. She has bubbles on her head and her blue hair curls underneath, making her head look like bubblegum ice-cream. I love how Mum had blue hair – you could never lose her in a crowd. There's another with all three of us the day they brought me home from the hospital. I look like a wrinkled little prune, but Mum and Dad look so happy. They must have been hoping for a prune-kid.

But the one I love most is of Mum chained to the big grey ironbark tree in Brennan Park. She looks so young and so passionate. The photo must have been taken when she was yelling something; her mouth's frozen wide open and her eyebrows are creased together in the middle of her forehead. There are lots of other students around her, but they might as well be out of focus with the way Mum just shines out of the middle of the photo. And right next to it, blu-tacked to the wall, is Mum's favourite quote. It's based off something written by Edmund Burke, who's some really old Irish guy with funny hair.

THE ONLY THING NECESSARY FOR THE TRIUMPH OF EVIL IS FOR GOOD MEN TO DO NOTHING.

But I crossed out 'men' and put 'people' because, you know, it's not the 18th century anymore, Mr Burke!

I drag myself off the bed as the laksa sloshes around, and head over to Mum's recipe card box. This is where all her 'thoughts' are kept. The label on the front is starting to curl up at the edges and the ink is fading, but the neat handwriting still clearly reads, 'TRIXIE WU'S THOUGHTS ON . . .'

I thumb my way through the cards. I don't really need advice right now. I just want to hear her voice. I stop at one I haven't read in a while.

Trixie Wu's Thoughts On . . .

ICE CREAM

Let me save you some time, Casey. Hokey pokey is the best. This is not an opinion, it's a fact. Your father loves peppermint choc-chip and it's something I will never understand about him. I wonder what your favourite will be. Whatever it is, eat lots of it (no matter what your dad says).

xMum

Hokey pokey is my favourite too. I slide the card back into its spot and turn to face my mirror.

I don't look like Mum. I wish I did, but I have Dad's hair and his eyes. I lean in closer and examine my face. I can't see Mum in there anywhere, no matter how hard I look. Once, when I was about four, Dad came into my room to find me painting my hair with blue wall paint that I'd found in the garage. I told him I wanted the same colour hair as Mum. What I got instead was a really short haircut.

I may not look like Mum, but I *can* try to follow in her footsteps. I turn away from the mirror and go to Dad's room to borrow his laptop.

Grandpa's snores drift up the stairs. He sounds like a moose with a snotty nose. I'm glad I don't have to share a bedroom with him. I'd never get any sleep. He shares with Dad instead, because at least Dad can turn his hearing aids off. Dad calls it 'selective hearing'.

I lean over the railing. Grandpa's asleep in his armchair with his head tipped all the way back, facing the ceiling. His mouth's wide open. I can't resist. I duck into the bathroom to grab a few tissues. Screwing them into balls, I toss them over the rail one by one, aiming for Grandpa's mouth. The first three miss. The fourth one bounces off his shiny forehead and onto the ground. But the fifth one hits his nose and bounces into his mouth. I wait for him to cough and splutter awake, but instead he just gives a big moose-like snore and the tissue ball shoots up into the air like a rocket.

Not what I expected.

Disappointed, I grab Dad's laptop from his room and head back to mine, shutting the door to block out the moose-man downstairs. Setting up the laptop on my desk, I check out a few of my go-to sites like *Treehugger* and *Millennium Kids*, and then finally click over to *What's On In Watterson* for some local news. The first headline stops my scrolling.

MAYOR LUPPHOL VISITS LOCAL SCHOOL

MAYOR LUPPHOL WILL BE VISITING LOCAL SCHOOL WATTERSON PRIMARY TO TALK TO KIDS ABOUT HER EXCITING 'MOVE WATTERSON INTO THE

FUTURE' ACTION PLAN, DETAILING THE NEW INITIATIVES SHE WILL BE BRINGING TO THEIR TOWN AND TO THEIR FUTURE. LOCAL MEDIA WILL ALSO ATTEND AS THE MAYOR REVEALS HER MAJOR CAMPAIGN POLICIES AND PLANS LEADING UP TO THE APPROACHING ELECTION.

This. Is. BRILLIANT. The mayor. Local media. It's the perfect time and place for our next big event. I open my email and paste the link. In the subject line, I write 'GREEN PEAS: The perfect opportunity'. I address it to zeketheninja@buzzmail.com (yes, Zeke is the only person in the world with a Buzzmail account) and cookie.munsta88@gmail.com and press SEND.

I wait. And wait. Dad says my generation has no patience, but I've waited a whole minute now for the Green Peas to respond and there's been no *BING* from my email.

A light flickers across the computer screen. I spin around to see Zeke standing in his bedroom window, shining a torch into my room. Zeke's bedroom window faces right onto mine. There's no escaping him. I go over to the window, holding my hand up to shield my eyes from his stupid torch-light. He drops the torch and holds up a piece of paper that he's written on in texta.

WHAT'S THE PLAN?

He's so annoying. Why can't he just answer me like a normal person? I make a typing gesture and mouth, 'Email me'.

He shakes his head, scribbles something on another piece of paper and holds it up. It reads . . .

ELECTRONIC COMMUNICATION NOT SAFE.

He writes something on the other side and holds it up again.

GREEN PEAS RULE 4: STAY OFF THE GRID

I shake my head at him, grab a pad and write my own message.

NEW RULE: YOU'RE AN IDIOT

He smiles and scribbles back.

NO. I'M A NINJA.

I throw the pad at the window and go back to the computer. I have an answer from Cookie. At least one of my friends is a rational human being. I click on the little envelope and read Cookie's message.

I'm guessing Zeke is answering by Morse code but I'm in! Meet at Brennan Park before school tmrw?

I type my response. Zeke is cc-ed in. I'm not making any extra effort than that.

Confirmed. 8 am. See you there.

I shut down the computer and check on Grandpa. He's still in his chair doing his best moose impression. A little disappointed with the outcome of my earlier tissue prank, this seems like the perfect opportunity to get one up on Grandpa.

And a good prankster never lets an opportunity pass. I go downstairs, grab a texta off the kitchen bench and carefully draw cat whiskers and a black nose on Grandpa's face.

'That's for the Oreo,' I say as I snap the lid back on and go to my room. Stuck to the outside of my bedroom window is a note reading,

SEE YOU AT 8 AM. FROM THE NINJA.

I look at the drop below. I look over to Zeke's window. We are both on the second floor with a good six metres separating us. How is that even possible?

Like most things when it comes to Zeke, I find it best not to try to understand. I set my alarm clock for 7 am, say goodnight to Mum and go to sleep.

GREEN PEAS RULE 5

Take every opportunity to make a difference.

Grandpa banging his way around the kitchen wakes me up before my alarm even rings. Because he's deaf, he's super unaware of the commotion he makes in the morning. Dad would've got home from work at about 5 am and taken his hearing aids out. A gorilla could fart through a loudspeaker next to his head and he'd sleep right through it. For me, however, come every Scrabble tournament day, Grandpa is my human alarm clock.

I go downstairs. Grandpa sounds like he's playing the percussion section of an orchestra with the pots and pans. I've told him a million times I'm happy with cereal for breakfast, but I can already smell the kaya toast and rice porridge cooking.

As Grandpa slices the bread, I sit down at the other end of the kitchen counter and knock on it so it vibrates and he knows I'm here. He spins around to face me and I try to stop myself from bursting out laughing. His texta whiskers fold upwards as he grins at me.

'Morning, Casey-poo! Hungry?' he asks.

I guess he hasn't looked in the mirror yet this morning. I secretly hope he doesn't check his reflection before he heads out for his Tuesday Scrabble tournament with his friends.

'Just toast, thanks, Ah Gong. No porridge.'

He nods and pops some on a plate. 'You're up early this morning.' He cuts a square of butter and drops it on top. I wait for him to put the toast in front of me and watch as the butter melts into the sweet coconut jam and bread.

'I'm meeting Cookie and Zeke before school. We're working on a . . . project together.' My mouth's already watering, but I have to wait for the butter to totally melt or it's just not the same.

'*Oooohhhh*, sounds very mysterious,' says Grandpa, his texta whiskers twitching as he speaks.

'Not really,' I say. I do my best to be nonchalant. This is my new favourite word. It sounds so exotic. And, weirdly, you can't be 'chalant'. You can only be the negative, with the 'non'. It's like a rebel word. The French really do have some great words. They also have chocolate croissants, so France seems like a place I'd like to visit.

Grandpa leans forward and whispers. 'Another Green Peas prank in the making?'

I frown at him. 'Ah Gong! What's the first rule?'

Grandpa straightens up. 'The first rule of Green Peas is . . .' He raises his finger to his lips. 'Shhhhhh.'

'Exactly,' I say.

I shovel my toast down and give Grandpa a kiss – being super careful to avoid any of his whiskers rubbing off on me.

Back upstairs, I quickly get ready, grab my stuff and sneak into Dad's room. He's fast asleep and his blanket has almost entirely made its way to the floor, so I cover him back up before I give him a peck on the cheek.

'See you tonight, Dad.' Then I run downstairs and off to Brennan Park.

Zeke's already waiting on Mum's bench. I pass by Kathy and give her a wave. She's cleaning her Lego house. 'Possum poop,' she explains. 'I love feeding them. Not so sure about the stinky little presents they leave me though.'

I take a seat next to Zeke and he passes me a book. It's used, and has a little red sticker on it that I recognise from the Watto Wears op shop. It's called *Words Of The World.*

'It's a whole book of all the coolest sounding words and their origins. You probably know a bunch already, but it's a pretty fat book so surely you can't know them all. I thought you might find it gratifying.'

I laugh. 'Did you get that word out of this book?'

'Maybe,' he says.

I flick through it. There's heaps in there I've never heard of. 'That's cool, Zeke. Thanks.'

'No worries.'

Cookie comes running up in a bright green t-shirt that reads, 'GREEN IS THE NEW BLACK'. 'Sorry, guys. It was crazy at home this morning. Dad was running late. Aaron's car wouldn't start. Our washing machine leaked all over the laundry floor. The cat threw up. And I couldn't find matching shoes.'

We look down at Cookie's feet. She's wearing one red sneaker and one blue sneaker. It's not the first time I've seen it.

'Oh,' I say. 'I kind of thought that was your thing. Some kind of arty fashion statement or something. Like how you always wear your t-shirts over your uniform.'

She thinks for a second. 'Hmm, well, maybe now it is.'

'You totally pull it off,' says Zeke.

'Sweet. Thanks,' she says, and takes a seat next to him. 'So what's the plan?' I pass her the Green Peas folder and she opens it up, her pen hovering over the page, ready to take notes. Cookie has way better handwriting than me. 'I'm guessing they'll do some sort of assembly or something for the mayor.'

'For sure,' I say. 'Let's start with a list of all the things we want to say, and then we'll decide which one is the most important. With the media there, this might be Green Peas' biggest event yet.'

A few hours later, we sit together as Mrs Keiren gets up to make the big announcement. She looks so pleased with herself; her chest is all puffed up and she's strutting around the stage as we get settled. Her boofy hair sticks up from her head in a puffy mohawk. It's like she's *trying* to look like a chicken.

Cookie pulls out her drawing pad, quickly sketching something. She slides it over towards us.

It's a Mrs Keiren rooster strutting back and forth across the stage.

I put my hand over my mouth to stop a laugh escaping.

Next to me, Zeke starts a quiet *bwark bwark bwark bwark*.

Now I'm losing it. I start to giggle.

Cookie pokes me with her pencil, but she's giggling too.

Other kids start to cluck and it spreads throughout the hall. Just quietly at first, but soon most of Year Six is clucking and Year Five is catching on.

Mrs Keiren spins around and the hall falls silent. Eying us off like we're juicy worms, she stomps to the microphone.

'Now listen here, every one of you.' She grips the side of the lectern and glares at the entire student body. 'Thursday is a very special day for this school. As many of you may already know, Mayor Lupphol will be visiting and I expect you all to be on your best behaviour. I do not want even a single hair on your head out of place, let alone any of the shenanigans that have been going on here recently.'

I scribble down 'shenanigans' in my folder. Great sounding word, even coming from Principal Chicken's Beak.

'This is an opportunity to show Watterson what well-behaved, quiet and obedient children we have at this school.'

The hairs on my neck stand up. Obedient? What does she think this is? A puppy training school? I think about Mum's favourite-word card . . .

Trixie Wu's Thoughts On . . .

WORDS

Learn AS MANY as you can. What you have to say matters, and the more words you know, the better you can say it. Read. Read a lot. Think. Think a lot. Then speak, and be heard. Some of my favourite words . . .

CONTEMPLATE

ZEALOUS

SERENDIPITOUS

DEFIANT

EPIPHANY

INCENDIARY

TENACIOUS

And my favourite of all . . .

CASEY ☺

xMum

I run over Mum's favourite words in my head. Obedient is not one of them. But defiant is.

'To celebrate and welcome the mayor, the entire school will attend a presentation on the bottom oval. We will listen to the mayor talk about her plans for the future of our town – YOUR future! At the end we'll be organising something very special for both the mayor and the media that will be attending. I saw it at an American Football game, and it didn't look that complicated.'

Mrs Keiren points a remote at the screen behind her and a video plays, showing a crowd on tiered seating at a school football game. On cue, each person in the crowd holds up either a red or white card, and as the edges all join together it spells out 'TIGERS FOR THE WIN!'.

I look at the kids around me. A big majority look half asleep, a couple are picking their noses and the rest are either writing notes to each other or reading comics on their laps. How Mrs Keiren thinks she's going to organise these kids to pull *that* off by Thursday is beyond me.

'Of course, this is just an example. We will spell out a lovely message to the mayor that will be captured by the media and no doubt be used in the upcoming campaign for re-election. Watterson Primary will be famous!'

She throws her hands in the air, expecting some response from us. But other than a few forced claps from the teachers, no one's overly impressed. It doesn't slow her down though. She has enough enthusiasm for her own idea that our encouragement clearly isn't required.

'Mr Deery will be in charge of organising the display and our art teacher, Mr Dinesh, will create and provide the materials.'

I can see from the looks on the two teachers' faces that this is the first they've heard of it. They turn to each other with eyes and mouths wide open.

Mrs Keiren pays zero attention to their confusion as she points at the screen. 'You just need to do the same thing as this . . . but instead the message should read –' She points her clicker at the screen and it flicks over to show the words:

MAYOR LUPPHOL, WATTERSON HERO!

I hear Cookie groan next to me.

Mrs Keiren smiles proudly. 'Mr Deery and Mr Dinesh will put together a team of students to help them, and anyone who volunteers will be excused from class for the first half of the day. The entire school will meet on the bottom oval at lunchtime to do a run-through. That is all.'

I stare at the words on the screen. I remember what Grandpa said about anagrams during Scrabble last night – his words echoing in my head in a very Yoda-like fashion.

Let the letters speak to you.

I write the phrase – 'MAYOR LUPPHOL, WATTERSON HERO!' – down carefully in my folder and study each letter. And then the letters don't just speak to me, they YELL! I've got it! The ultimate prank. But it's going to take some work.

Mr Dinesh and Mr Deery are huddled together at the front of the hall, looking pretty stressed about the responsibility that's just been dumped in their laps. I elbow Cookie in the ribs. 'Go volunteer to help Mr Dinesh.'

She looks at me, confused. 'Okay, but what do you want –'

'Just go,' I say, shoving her out of the row. 'I'll explain later.' I grab Zeke's arm and drag him behind me. 'C'mon, Zeke, Mr Deery needs our help.'

By the time we squeeze our way through all the kids trying to leave, Mrs Keiren has joined the two teachers.

'But Mrs Keiren,' explains Mr Deery, 'I honestly don't know how I'm supposed to organise that. And by lunchtime? I mean it's not very –'

'Use an app or something,' Mrs Keiren snaps at him. 'Isn't that what you teachers do these days? Back in my day it was blackboards. Do you even know what they are?'

'Yes, Mrs Keiren, I know what they are,' he sighs. 'But we've moved onto interactive whiteboards now, remember?'

'Perfect!' she yells. 'Then use that! And be ready for rehearsal with the entire school at lunchtime.'

'But I'm not sure that's possible,' says Mr Deery.

'That's not the "can do" Watterson attitude I'm looking for,' Mrs Keiren says, turning a shade of purple. 'You have six hundred children. So six hundred cards. Just make it spell the message in school colours, tell Mr Dinesh what to paint, then get the children to hold it up. Easy!' She waves her hands in the air like she's doing magic. 'Your classes are being covered. See you at lunch!'

With that she storms off, leaving Mr Dinesh and Mr Deery looking at each other like lost puppies. They definitely need our help.

'Mr Deery! Zeke can totally help you with this. You know what a tech head he is.' I shove Zeke forward to stand in front of Mr Deery. 'Right, Zeke?'

He looks at me in confusion but rolls with it. 'Um, yeah sure. So we could, um . . .' He stops for a moment, and I'm worried that maybe he doesn't have a solution. What's the use of having a genius friend if he can't be a genius on cue? 'Actually, yeah, all we need to do is create a grid divided into six hundred squares. No wait!' Zeke holds his finger in the air, mumbling as he calculates a few gazillion sums. 'Actually, let's do 1200 squares, and everyone can hold two each, otherwise there's no way it'll all fit. We're not exactly working with an American football crowd here.'

'Or an American football budget,' mumbles Mr Deery.

Zeke continues. 'Then we write the message Mrs Keiren wants onto the grid and that will give us the design that Mr Dinesh needs. We paint the squares blue or white, according to the grid, then just hand them out to kids in the grid order. Simple!'

Mr Deery and Mr Dinesh look at each other again. The lost puppy looks remain.

'It doesn't sound simple,' says Mr Deery.

Zeke flashes a smile. 'It is, I promise. I'll show you.'

Cookie steps forward. 'And I'll help you with the cards, Mr Dinesh.'

I step forward. 'I can help too. Just to lend an extra hand.'

The teachers smile at us. 'Thanks, kids. We really appreciate it.'

'No problem at all. Happy to help out for such an important event,' I say.

Cookie grabs Mr Dinesh. 'See you soon?' She shrugs at me, I give her the thumbs-up and she drags the baffled teacher towards the art room.

'Where to?' asks Mr Deery.

'The computer room,' says Zeke. Mr Deery nods and we follow him.

Staying just far enough behind Mr Deery that he can't hear us, Zeke whispers to me 'Want to tell me the plan?'

'I'm still making it,' I say, my brain churning away like Grandpa making durian ice-cream.

Mr Deery has zero idea what Zeke's doing on the computer. He's looking at the screen like it's an alien about to suck his brains out.

'How do you know how to do all this, Zeke?' Mr Deery says, clearly impressed.

'Mum's obsessed with pretty much anything tech-y. Our entire house is covered with her gadgets and the bits and pieces she collects or buys off the internet. So I get to play around with spare computer parts and cameras and all kinds of cool stuff,' Zeke says. 'I guess I sort of inherited her knack for it.'

I watch carefully as Zeke uses an online generator to create a grid that's twenty-five squares by forty-eight squares. I'm just going to trust Zeke that it equals 1200, because I would definitely need a calculator to confirm. 'You know he even built his own robot once?' I tell Mr Deery.

'Really, Zeke?' he says. 'That's amazing! What did it do?'

'I made it from a vacuum robot, but connected it to an old iPhone. Then I connected the "Find My Phone" app to my brother's phone so it would just follow him around the house everywhere he went. It even went into the toilet with him.'

I nod at Mr Deery. 'Yeah, seriously, he spent a whole week making a robot just to annoy his brother.'

Mr Deery laughs. 'If only you used your powers for good, Zeke!'

Zeke and I look at each other. I wish we could tell him we *are* using our powers for good. I really like Mr Deery – I mean, everyone likes Mr Deery – and

I actually think he would make a great member of Green Peas, but I'm just not sure he's ready yet. He still has so much to learn.

'What was the sign supposed to say again?' Zeke asks.

Mr Deery pulls out his phone and brings up the photo he took of Mrs Keiren's presentation. He lets out a small groan and can barely say the words. 'MAYOR LUPPHOL, WATTERSON HERO!' Mr Deery's nose screws up like he just smelt something bad.

'Is that what you want us to write, Mr Deery?' I ask.

He pauses. 'It's not really up to me.'

I can tell he's doing that adult thing where he doesn't like something but he's too polite – or maybe too scared – to say so.

'Do you think the mayor will get re-elected again?' I ask.

Mr Deery sighs. 'Probably. There's no one running against her . . . again. Same problem we have every year – everyone else has dropped out. So that doesn't give the voters a lot of options.'

'Maybe you should run, Mr Deery,' suggests Zeke. 'You'd make a great mayor.'

Mr Deery laughs. 'I have no interest in being involved in politics at all, thank you, Zeke.'

'But isn't that the problem?' I ask. 'None of the people we need in charge want to be in charge?'

Mr Deery stares at me like I'm as confusing as the computer. 'That's um . . . I guess . . .'

You would think teachers would be better at completing sentences.

Mr Deery gives up and turns back to the computer. 'So how's this going to work, Zeke?'

Zeke has written Mrs Keiren's message across the grid in blue, and numbered the squares 1–1200. Now he transfers the information over to a spreadsheet that lists the card number and what colour it needs to be.

'It's simple,' says Zeke. 'Just get Mr Dinesh to make you 1200 squares. Four hundred and fifty-six of them need to be blue, the rest white. The kids then stand in a rectangle like the grid and you just hand the cards out to the kids according to this spreadsheet.' Zeke taps on the screen.

'See, first kid gets one blue, one white. Second kid, two whites and so on. When they each hold their two cards up, it'll spell it out just like this!' He taps the screen.

Mr Deery shakes his head. 'Zeke, you're a genius!'

'Actually I'm a ninja.'

'Huh?' says Mr Deery.

'Nothing!' I say, glaring at Zeke.

Zeke prints out both the grid and the spreadsheet. I beat Mr Deery over to the printer. 'I can take these to Mr Dinesh for you if you like?' I offer. 'Zeke and I can give him and Cookie a hand while we're there.'

Mr Deery gives me a warm smile. 'Thanks, Casey. And you too, Zeke. You really saved my neck on this one. Sometimes I think Mrs Keiren forgets I'm just a little ol' teacher, not a graphic-design whiz.'

'You're not JUST a teacher,' I say. 'You're a really good one. I'm glad Mr Bijac had a baby and you had to fill in.'

'Aw, thanks, Casey,' says Mr Deery. 'I'm glad he had a baby too.'

'I bet he's not glad,' says Zeke. 'Nappies stink!'

Mr Deery leaves the computer room and Zeke goes to stand up. I put my hand on his shoulder and push him back down into the seat.

'Not so fast there, ninja-boy,' I say. 'You've got one more spreadsheet to make.'

Zeke grins up at me as his hands hover over the keyboard. 'What've you got in mind, boss?'

I pull up a seat next to Zeke and explain to him what I need.

GREEN PEAS RULE 6

BE CLEVER. A CLEVER PRANK IS A GOOD PRANK.

I can hear the commotion coming from the art room before we even walk through the doors. When I push them open, Mr Dinesh is running around waving his arms in the air like a Kermit the Frog GIF. His face is weirdly pink and I think he might have forgotten how to breathe. Adults get stressed about anything. It looks like Cookie has managed to find a few more kids to help, but at the moment they're just standing around watching Mr Dinesh's Kermit impression with confusion. As Cookie sees us walk in, a look of relief washes over her face and she runs over.

'Am I glad you guys are here! I think something has short-circuited in Mr Dinesh's brain,' says Cookie. 'He's been running around like this for the last twenty minutes, and all that we've managed to achieve is a pile of square paper awaiting instructions. Please tell me you have a plan.'

I hold up the spreadsheets with a grin. 'Sure do,' I say. 'In fact, I have two!' I hand the original papers to Zeke. 'Why don't you take these to Mr Dinesh, try to get him to stand in one spot for five minutes and explain how it all works.'

Zeke nods and takes the papers. 'In the meantime, Cookie and I will take a look at these ones.' I wave the second lot of papers in Cookie's face.

'Roger that!' says Zeke, and heads over to Mr Dinesh.

Cookie and I slink off to the corner of the art room. 'After the rehearsal today goes super smoothly, I need you to switch Mr Dinesh's spreadsheet with this one.' I pass her the paper.

'Too easy. So what's the difference?' she asks.

I show her the second grid Zeke and I printed up. 'A slight adjustment to the wording of the message.'

Cookie's eyes light up. 'I love it!'

'Let's hope Mrs Keiren and the mayor and the media feel the same.'

Cookie laughs. 'You know they won't. Now, let's get to work.'

Zeke has explained the plan to Mr Dinesh, who has now stopped the circling and arm-waving, and his face has returned to its natural colour. A bunch of kids have already started painting blue squares, so Cookie and I start counting out the white ones to set aside.

By lunchtime everything is dry and the squares have been sorted, ready to hand out in the order of the spreadsheet. When we get to the oval, Mr Deery has already put all the kids in their lines.

Mr Dinesh runs his finger down the spreadsheet and we hand out the cardboard squares as instructed. 'Blue and white. White and white. White and blue.'

Mrs Keiren stands at the top of the ramp leading down to the oval so she can get a good bird's-eye view. Apparently the stage will also be set up there so the mayor will be looking down on us kids. It's hard to ignore the metaphor. (I learnt 'metaphor' from *Words of the World*. It has Greek origins, like all good words – and good baklava – do.)

'All right, children,' Mrs Keiren screeches through the sports teacher's megaphone. 'Hold both your cards in front of you and on the count of three, everyone lift their cards above their heads, making sure the edges touch the person next to you.'

Mr Deery and Mr Dinesh stand next to her, looking pretty nervous. Zeke, Cookie and I – and the rest of the helpers – are with the teachers, keen to get a good view of our work.

'Three, two, one!'

The kids all hold up their blue and white squares and there, spelled out clearly, is Mrs Keiren's message, 'MAYOR LUPPHOL, WATTERSON HERO!' Mr Dinesh and Mr Deery both let out a relieved sigh. Mrs Keiren claps her hands together, 'Excellent, just excellent!'

Us Green Peas allow ourselves a little fist bump as we look over our handiwork.

Mr Deery bends down to whisper to us. 'Thanks, kids. You saved our skins.'

'Anytime, Mr Deery,' I say, and offer him a fist bump. He just looks at it, confused, and gives my fist a weird sort of high five. Lucky Mr Deery's such a good teacher, because he's not winning any cool points, that's for sure.

Mrs Keiren puts the megaphone back up to her beak and continues squawking.

'Excellent work, students! The mayor and the media will love this. Please hand your cards back to the helpers as you leave, and enjoy the rest of your lunch.'

We help collect the cards and take them back to the art room.

'Great rehearsal,' says Mr Dinesh. 'Let's hope it's that successful on Thursday.'

'Let's hope!' I say, but I'm pretty sure we have VERY different ideas of what successful looks like.

When I get home from school, Dad's in the kitchen.

'Where's Ah Gong?' I ask.

Dad drops a chicken thigh into a pan of soy sauce. 'Upstairs taking a nap. I don't have to start until eight tonight, so I'm going to cook.'

I make a note to self: check my room for booby traps. There's a much higher chance that Grandpa's up there putting fake vomit in my bed or a whoopee cushion on my chair than actually taking a nap.

'Is that your honey and soy chicken?' I ask.

He winks at me. 'Sure is. Although technically it's your mum's. I stole the recipe from her.'

'First meal she ever cooked for you,' I say. I think I've heard almost every story about Mum but I never get tired of them. In our family, we call them Trixie-tales and it's because of them that I feel like I know Mum so well.

Mum and Dad met in university. It was Open Day and the uni had set up all these stands on the campus. Mum was trying to get people to sign up for the environmental group and Dad was joining the 'Future Leaders' because he wanted to get into politics. They ended up getting into a big argument about the best way to change the world for the better. The argument turned into coffee, the coffee turned into dinner and the rest is history.

Dad's security uniform hangs near the ironing board. 'Do you want me to iron that for you, Dad?'

'Sure, thanks, hon.'

I put his dark pants on the board and run the iron over them. 'Do you like being a security guard, Dad?'

He throws another thigh in the pan and shrugs. 'It's okay. The hours mean I get to be here when you come home from school. Lots of time to myself to listen to podcasts.'

'But Ah Gong says you wanted to be Prime Minister when you were young. What happened?'

Dad jiggles the handle of the frying pan. 'Lots of things,' he says. 'My hearing got worse. And then your mum got sick. We had a big talk about how I might end up being a single dad, and we decided something a bit more stable would be better for the whole family.' He taps my nose with his soy sauce finger. 'Your mum was a smart person, Casey. She knew what was best for us.'

I wipe the sauce off my nose. 'But you could have made a real difference, Dad.'

He leans his palms on the kitchen bench. 'I did, Casey. I made you.' He gives me a kiss on the forehead and goes back to the chicken.

I think about one of Mum's cards. It's one she wrote before I was born, and I've never really understood it.

Trixie Wu's Thoughts On . . .

SACRIFICE

We give up a lot of things in this world. Some for the better. Some for the worse. But all of them are hard to let go of.

Trixie

'Are you making Trixie's chicken?' yells Grandpa, and I hear his footsteps on the stairs. 'You never make it quite as good as she did, you know?'

'Gee, thanks,' says Dad as he adds some honey to the sauce.

The doorbell rings and the red light flashes. 'I'll get it,' says Grandpa, and disappears down the hallway. 'Look what the cat dragged in, Casey.'

Zeke follows Grandpa into the kitchen. 'Hi, Casey. Hi, Mr Wu.'

I give him a wave and Dad holds out the chicken. 'Hi, Zeke. Staying for dinner? There's plenty to go around.' Zeke looks at me.

'If you want,' I say. 'Dad's chicken's pretty great.'

'Thank you, Casey,' says Dad, and turns to Grandpa. 'See!'

'Yes, but she doesn't remember how good it was when Trixie made it.'

It's true. I don't remember. I wish I did. But I still think Dad makes it great, and I love that Mum taught him.

'Thanks, Mr Wu,' says Zeke. 'I'd love to stay.'

'Do you want to call your mum and let her know?' asks Dad, passing Zeke his mobile phone.

'I'll just text her,' he says, and types a message into the phone. 'How's work going, Mr Wu?'

Dad looks at Zeke with surprise. 'How nice of you to ask, Zeke.' Dad shoots me a look. Zeke's such a suck-up!

'Dad! I literally JUST asked you about your job.'

He turns deliberately to Zeke. 'It's going well, thank you, Zeke.'

I put Dad's shirt on the hanger with his pants. 'Yeah, he's really churning through those podcasts.'

Dad throws a tea towel at me, which I duck from with the reflexes of a . . . nooooo, I nearly said ninja! I've been spending way too much time with Zeke.

Dad turns back to Zeke. 'I'll have you know, there's actually been a bit of action at the Mall lately. The night security cameras caught some illegal dumping. We got the guy on video. And his blue ute. We haven't caught him yet, but I am on the case!'

'Go, Detective Dad!' I say sarcastically. 'Maybe stick to your honey and soy chicken and leave this one to the cops?'

Dad turns the chicken over. 'Henry Wu, world's most underestimated father.'

Zeke nods at Dad in sympathy. 'I hear ya, Mr Wu.' He jabs his thumb in my direction. 'No faith in us, that one. No faith at all.'

'What are they saying?' asks Grandpa, unable to follow the conversation from the dining room table.

I shake my head and face him. 'Be happy you can't hear this one, Ah Gong.'

He frowns at me. 'I wouldn't have asked if I was happy not to know.'

A pang of shame jabs me like a fork in the ribs. I know better than that. I pull out the chair opposite Grandpa and sit facing him.

'You ready to have the world's most eye-rolling conversation relayed to you?' I ask.

He nods. 'You know me, Casey-poo. Always up for a good eye-roll.'

'Well, with these two,' I say, pointing my thumb over my shoulder towards Zeke and Dad, 'eye-rolls are guaranteed.'

Grandpa pushes his crossword aside as I relay the conversation, being careful not to leave out any of the annoying details. And Grandpa enjoys every eye-rolling moment of it.

GREEN PEAS RULE 7

Go for maximum exposure and maximum effect.

On Thursday morning, I am pumped. The whole school's buzzing about the mayor's visit. The teachers because, well, it's the mayor. The kids because there are TV crews and cameras at our school and let's be honest, what kid doesn't want to get on TV?

Actually, the answer is me. I'm all about being clandestine today – another word from Zeke's book. It sounds like a fancy breed of poodle, but it just means totes super-spyish.

Green Peas meet before school to run over the plan one last time. Zeke and I are in charge of reordering the squares before the handout, and Cookie has to make the spreadsheet switch.

'You don't think this one's going to bring a whole lot of attention to us?' says Cookie.

'Maybe,' I say. 'But maybe it'll be worth it.'

'Plus,' Zeke says, 'there are so many kids helping out it will be hard to pin it to us.'

Cookie shakes her head. 'Zeke, YOU made the spreadsheet. You don't think that's a dead giveaway?'

'Yeah, but you carried the squares, and Casey handed them out, and Joel painted them, and Yawanda sorted them and Lucy put them in order. And more importantly, Mr Deery organised the kids and Mr Dinesh read out the spreadsheet.' Zeke raises his eyebrows. 'There's a lot of moments where this could've turned.'

I nod. 'And hopefully they'll be so busy dealing with the repercussions, they won't have time to work it out.'

'Oooohhhh, repercussions. Good word!' says Zeke.

'Thanks! Found it in this book I got.' I grin. 'Ready to do this?'

'READY!' say Cookie and Zeke. And with that, we go into battle.

Trixie Wu's Thoughts On . . .

BRAVERY

It comes in many forms and means many things. But I like to think of it like Dr Robert Anthony: 'The opposite of bravery is not cowardice but conformity.'

Trixie

A big stage has been built at the top of the ramp to the bottom oval, and a huge screen fills the backdrop. Cameras and reporters hover around, and even a bunch of parents and locals have turned up. I told Zeke we probably didn't need to film this one with all the media being there, but he said it's always good to have your own footage. I'm not sure where he put his GoPros, but he says he's 'got it covered'.

Mr Deery and Mr Dinesh are back to being all nervous and jumpy, running around double-checking everything. Lucky it's not too hot today, because the whole school has been down here waiting for a while now.

Mrs Keiren's on stage with Mayor Lupphol. The principal buzzes around her, pointing things out and flapping her arms. Mayor Lupphol smiles politely, but the tension in her jaw tells me she's gritting her teeth behind that smile. The mayor edges away from Mrs Keiren and over to a woman on the side wearing a dark suit. They're discussing something, but I can't hear what from here.

'Do we actually get to meet the mayor?' asks Zeke.

Mr Deery shakes his head. 'No. Mrs Keiren offered to show her around the school but she wasn't interested. I even offered to introduce her to Coco and Buggy. She looked like she'd rather clean out their cage with her tongue.'

Coco and Buggy are our school guinea pigs. I can't imagine ANYONE not loving them. They are the cutest, fattest, squishiest animals on the planet.

Mr Dinesh elbows Mr Deery. 'Maybe she's just not an animal person?'

Mr Deery makes a funny snorting sound and mumbles under his breath. 'Yeah, maybe.'

Mrs Keiren waves at us from the stage and Mr Deery springs into action. 'Okay, everybody good to go?' he asks. All the helpers nod. We line up, holding our squares.

Mr Dinesh taps his clipboard with the spread-sheet attached. 'Good to go!' he says.

Mr Deery gives him a thumbs-up. 'All right. Well, the kids are in place, so why don't you start handing everything out?'

I shoot Cookie a quick look and she nods. The switch has already been made.

We follow Mr Dinesh's instructions and hand out the blue and white squares in the order indicated on his spreadsheet.

Doof, doof, doof.

Mrs Keiren bangs on the microphone. 'Okay, everyone, your attention, please. Put your hands together for our distinguished guest, Mayor Lupphol.'

We all clap as the mayor steps towards the microphone. She isn't as tall as Mrs Keiren, so she drags the microphone down to meet her mouth. She looks very . . . put together. Like it takes her a long time to get ready in the morning. Her skin's pulled tight over high cheekbones. Her hair's yanked back with not a single strand escaping from the bun perched on the back of her head. My hair would never look like that. When I do a ponytail, the bits at the front and back escape the hairband within five seconds of me tying it back and behave like I've been electrocuted. Maybe that's what you need to be the mayor – very well-behaved hair?

'It's a pleasure to be here today,' the mayor says into the microphone. Her voice is as strong and certain as her hairdo, not a word out of place. 'I cannot imagine a better audience to talk to about my "Move Watterson into the Future" project than the actual future of Watterson. You!'

As she says it, she stabs a long, bony finger towards us. I think it's supposed to be motivational, but it looks more like she's accusing us of something.

'Watterson has spent too many years as a small town. We can be bigger and better. I will move Watterson into the 21st century with development that means you, the future of Watterson, will have a bustling and profitable mini-city that you will want to *stay* in. A city full of opportunities and development. A city where . . .'

I'm not the only one starting to tune out, and I think the mayor knows it. She goes on for a bit longer with something along the lines of . . .

'Importance of progress *blah blah blah* change and growth *blah blah blah* develop into a thriving *blah blah blah*.'

The kids are starting to squirm. Mrs Keiren is starting to fume. The mayor looks to the lady in the dark suit, who points to the screen.

'Let's take a look at our plans for the future of Watterson!' says the mayor, and swings her arm behind her. Dark-suit lady presses a button and the screen flashes to life.

The video is very impressive. Completely confusing, but impressive. There are swirling graphics and 3D models of buildings I don't recognise in places I do. There's some futuristic-sounding lady's voice telling us that all this stuff (whatever it is) is going to make Watterson 'the place to be'. I'm pretty sure I even saw a flying car in there at some point. By the end of it, I have zero idea of what exactly the mayor's planning to do, but I feel officially 'dazzled'. Judging by the faces around me, I'm not the only one.

I lean over to Cookie and whisper. 'Wait, so where's the new shopping centre going? And how many new apartments in the next five years?'

Cookie shrugs. 'All I know is according to that video, Watterson will look like Dubai by the time Mayor Lupphol's finished with it.'

'Is that a good thing?' I ask.

'How would I know?' Cookie says. 'I haven't been to Dubai.'

Mr Dinesh gives us a gentle shove. 'Come on, kids, get ready.' He waves his hands in the air and all us kids shuffle together, making sure we're shoulder to shoulder.

The mayor's speaking again. 'So as you can see, I have big plans for the future of Watterson. I am going to make this town the place to be – bringing people and business and money to our town. You won't recognise this place when I'm done.'

I'm not sure I like the sound of that. I quite like Watterson. Okay, Watto Mall is kind of old and we don't have all the newest, fanciest stuff. The springs in the seats at Balthazar Theatre kind of poke you in the bum and the community hall smells like possum poop, but it's home. I'm not sure I need big apartment blocks and flying cars in my town.

Mrs Keiren takes over the microphone. 'We have organised a little surprise as a thank you, Mayor Lupphol, for coming to visit our school. The children have a message they would like to share with you, from the bottom of our Watterson Primary hearts.' The principal waves her hand out dramatically over all of us kids standing there, holding our squares. She double checks to make sure all the cameras are pointing at us and then, with a huge, cheesy smile, she counts down . . .

'Three, two, one . . .'

The six hundred kids of Watterson Primary hold up their blue and white squares. I watch as

Mrs Keiren's cheesy grin falls from her face and is replaced with the red-purple kettle-boiling face. She is not happy. I don't think the mayor is either.

The cameras roll. The crowd points. My chest fills up as I hear the passing comments.

'Does that say what I think?'

'Zoom in on that!'

'Do you think that was planned?'

'Get a close-up of the mayor's face.'

My stomach feels like a tumble dryer, but my poker-face remains.

This one's for you, Mum!

GREEN PEAS RULE 8

WHEN SOMETHING IS WRONG, TAKE ACTION.

Cookie, Zeke and I huddle outside our classroom, listening at the door. Inside, Mrs Keiren, Mr Dinesh and Mr Deery crowd around the class iPad.

'I'll put it up on the board,' says Mr Deery, tapping at the screen. I peer through the gap in the door. A frozen video flicks up onto the interactive whiteboard, showing a wide shot of the assembly for the mayor.

'How is it out there already?' yells Mrs Keiren.

Mr Deery shrugs. 'Things get up on YouTube pretty quickly these days. It's the beauty of the internet, I guess.' Mrs Keiren glares at him.

'What does it say below the video?' asks Mr Dinesh nervously.

Mr Deery reads the description. 'A visit to a local primary school by Mayor Lupphol goes awry when students take what appears to be a stand against the mayor's development plans for the city and, in fact, the planet.'

Mr Deery presses play and the video comes to life, the kids of Watterson Primary holding up squares to form the message . . .

STOP, MAYOR! HELP OUR EARTH NOW ☺

'Genius!' whispers Zeke.

'Thanks,' I say.

'How did you even figure out that was an anagram of "MAYOR LUPPHOL, WATTERSON HERO"?' asks Cookie.

'I play a lot of Scrabble with Grandpa,' I say. 'I just took the letters of the original message and spelt out something a little more . . . controversial. And made the extra 'L' into a smiley face for effect.'

'Like I said,' says Zeke. 'Genius!'

Genius. I like that word.

Inside the classroom, the teachers are not as happy. 'But how is it even possible?' asks Mr Deery. 'You saw the rehearsal. It went perfectly, and we did exactly the same thing.'

Mrs Keiren is still fuming. 'Give me that spreadsheet,' she says, snatching the clipboard out of Mr Dinesh's hands. I hold my breath. When they compare the spreadsheet to the grid, they'll see it doesn't match. They'll know it's been switched, and maybe even trace it back to us. The three teachers crowd around the clipboard, flicking back and forth between the pages.

'See!' says Mr Dinesh. 'It all matches. It makes no sense at all. How could it possibly have spelt out a different message?'

I breathe out, confused. 'But how . . .'

Zeke pulls some papers out of his back pocket and waves them at me. 'I switched them back.' He grins. 'Like a ninja.'

I'm impressed. I hadn't thought to do that. I'm not saying Zeke's a ninja, but that was a pretty stealth move.

'Who's the genius now?' says Cookie. I give Zeke a fist bump. I'm happy to share the title.

Mrs Keiren thumps the clipboard on the table. 'It's got to be the same brats who have been pulling all these other pranks.'

'But how?' says Mr Deery. 'The entire school, all six hundred kids, would have to be in on it to pull this off.'

Mrs Keiren's eyes narrow. 'Well, maybe they are. Maybe it's a conspiracy.'

Mr Dinesh looks at Mrs Keiren like she's losing it just a little. 'We're talking about primary school kids here, Mrs Keiren. They're not exactly the Illuminati.'

She stabs a finger in the air. 'Don't underestimate them,' she warns. 'They are sneaky and clever, and who knows what they're capable of when they gang up? I don't have to remind you about our little schoolyard millionaire situation at the beginning of the year, do I? They can be clever little monsters when they want to be.'

On the screen, the video continues to play, cutting from a shot of our message to a close-up of the mayor's face, looking furious.

'See!' says Mrs Keiren, pointing at the video. 'If they can organise this, they can do anything. Do you know how this makes me look? On YouTube, for everyone to see! I will not have my school be the laughing-stock of Watterson.' Mrs Keiren slams her fist on the table, making Mr Deery and Mr Dinesh jump. 'I want the entire staff on high alert. Find the ringleaders behind this and discipline them!'

Mr Deery sighs. 'Let's not get carried away. It was just a harmless prank. No one got hurt. They're only trying to make themselves heard.'

'Make themselves heard!' Mrs Keiren's voice goes up another decibel. 'Not on my time and not on my school grounds. They can save their little protests for their own backyards!'

Mr Deery rubs his forehead. 'Um, I think that would sort of defeat the purpose of a public protest?'

'Just find them!' she yells. The teachers head for the door and we make a run for it, bolting to a playground bench and quickly taking a seat.

'Well, at least they don't know who's behind it,' says Cookie.

'And let's keep it that way,' I say. 'Zeke, can you bring the footage over tonight?'

'Roger!'

'Why don't you both come over for dinner? Grandpa's making chicken rice. We can go through the footage together and edit our own video. I think this might be our biggest event yet.'

Cookie nods. 'Definitely, except –'

'Don't worry,' I say, putting my hand on Cookie's shoulder. 'Vego rice for you, Grandpa knows. Let's say five at my house?'

They both nod and head off. I stay on the bench for a bit. I think about Mum being chained to the tree in Brennan Park with her protest signs and her friends gathered around her. I wish she were here to see what I'd done. I think she'd be proud.

Trixie Wu's Thoughts On . . .

FOMO

This stands for Fear of Missing out. I have so much FOMO when it comes to you, Casey-baby. Your first day of school. Your first heartbreak. Your first success. Your first failure. I want so badly to be there for it all. Live life boldly, Casey. I love you.

xMum

The delicious smell of Grandpa's chicken rice wafts out into the lounge room, where we sit huddled around Zeke's laptop.

'We should open the video with a wide shot of the whole school,' I say.

'Nah,' says Cookie. 'Do a close-up of Mrs Keiren flapping about on the stage.'

Zeke moves the cursor around the screen. 'See, this here is why I normally do the editing part on my own.' He scrubs through some footage of the stage, playing it in reverse so Mrs Keiren looks like a chicken running in reverse. He moves the cursor backwards and forwards, getting her stuck in a loop. We all crack up laughing.

'Who wants some –' Grandpa walks into the lounge room but stops as he sees us rolling around on the couch. 'All right, what's going on here? What's so funny?'

Zeke looks up at Grandpa. 'Oh, we're just watching a funny video, Mr Wu. A little prank that was pulled at our school today.' Zeke always looks at Grandpa and speaks clearly for him. Not many people do it, even when I ask them to, but Zeke always does. It's probably part of the reason Grandpa likes him so much.

'The one with the mayor? Giuseppe told me about it when I was in town this afternoon.' Grandpa comes over and squeezes himself onto the couch next to us, pushing Cookie up onto the armrest. 'Can I watch it?'

'We're just looking at some bits before the prank at the moment. Just before the mayor gives her speech,' I say.

'That's fine,' he says. 'I want to see it all. I want to watch her miserable face when she gets the message that not everybody wants to live in a metropolis.' Grandpa squints at the screen.

'Clever little stunt, that one, wouldn't you say, kids? I'd sure like to give those responsible a good old handshake for stating their piece to that greedy money-grabber.'

Cookie and Zeke look at me. I look at Grandpa. But we ALL know the first rule.

'I'm sure they appreciate your support, Ah Gong. Don't they, guys?' Cookie and Zeke nod enthusiastically.

Grandpa smiles proudly. 'Well, I like their style. Now let's see the action.'

Zeke lets the video play. Mrs Keiren's still running around on stage, and the mayor's talking to the lady in the suit on the side.

'Fast forward through this bit, Zeke,' I say. 'Let's get to the fun part.'

Zeke puts his hand on the mouse but Grandpa stops him. 'Wait!' Grandpa leans closer to the screen. 'Who is that woman?'

'Dunno,' I say. 'Just one of the mayor's assistants or something, I guess.'

Grandpa looks at Zeke. 'Can you go in closer to them?'

'Like zoom in?' says Zeke. 'I can do even better. I have a close-up from another camera.'

He flicks over to another camera angle, which clearly shows the faces of the mayor and the mystery lady. They're looking out over the sea of kids, but evidently talking to each other about something far more interesting.

'Play it again,' says Grandpa. Zeke goes back a bit and lets the video replay. You can't hear what the mayor's saying – the camera's too far away to pick up their voices – so we just sit there in silence watching the two women mouthing something to each other and waving their hands around. Grandpa watches them carefully. 'One more time.' Zeke plays the clip again.

Finally Grandpa looks up at us. 'They're getting rid of Brennan Park?' he asks.

'WHAT?' we all say.

Grandpa points at the screen. 'That's what they're talking about. Well, I'm pretty sure that's the gist of it, at least. They're saying something about getting rid of Brennan Park.'

'But they can't do that,' says Cookie. She looks at me. 'Can they?'

My stomach goes tight and my ears start to heat up. Brennan Park is our park. Brennan Park is how we walk to school. Where we have our picnics. It has heaps of possums and Kathy's Lego house. It has the big grey ironbark tree and Mum's bench. And they want to get rid of it?

Over. My. Dead. Body.

'Who does she think she is?!' I explode as soon as we make it upstairs to my room.

I spent all of dinner fuming in silence. We would never make a Green Peas plan in front of Grandpa – that would totally destroy any plausible deniability – but now that we're finally upstairs, I blow up.

'We have to stop her! We need a plan. NOW!!!'

'Shhh. Keep your voice down,' says Zeke, pointing downstairs.

'Why?' I say, throwing my arms in the air. 'He's deaf!'

Zeke nods. 'Good point. Keep yelling.'

'She can't do this, right? I mean, even if she *is* the mayor. Surely there has to be a vote or something?'

Cookie shrugs. 'I don't know. But look, we don't really even know what's happening. Maybe your grandpa read their lips wrong. You say yourself it's a hard thing to do and not an exact science. Maybe he got it wrong. So let's just try to keep our cool and find out more about what's going on.'

'I agree,' says Zeke. 'I mean, no one can just get rid of a park, right? It's a public place. It'd have to go through a process and a committee would have to agree and the town would have to be okay with it and there's no way that Watterson would be okay with losing Brennan Park, no way.'

I start to calm down. They're right. I mean, she's the mayor, not the supreme ruler of the world. She can't just do whatever she likes. And why would anyone want to get rid of a park, anyway?

'Okay,' I say. 'You're right. Let's not panic yet. We'll find out some more info first.'

Cookie pulls a pencil from behind her ear. 'Sounds like we need a plan!'

'Absolutely!' I say. I get out the Green Peas folder and we all take a seat on the floor.

GREEN PEAS RULE 9

Be creative. Stay ahead of the game.

'Well, I'll have to run it past Mrs Keiren first, you know?' Mr Dinesh is getting the art room ready for his first class. 'And we don't have all the tools here to make a plaque.'

'That's okay,' says Cookie. 'I can make it. My dad has all the stuff we need at home, and Aaron can do the engraving for us.'

Our idea to make a plaque for the mayor – to say 'thank you', and mostly 'sorry', for the disruption the other day – has made Mr Dinesh nervous. But everything makes Mr Dinesh nervous. I thought all artists were super chill like Cookie, but Mr Dinesh is walking proof that artists come in all shapes, sizes and anxiety levels. We actually need to take care of making the plaque ourselves for our plan to work – but we do want to present it from the school to give it some legitimacy.

'I don't know,' says Mr Dinesh, twisting his fingers together nervously. 'Maybe we should just leave the mayor alone for a while.'

I jump in. 'What if we check what Mr Deery thinks?'

Mr Dinesh's eyes light up. 'Great idea! See what he says.' I can almost see him straighten up as the weight of the decision is catapulted in another teacher's direction.

'If he's okay with it, and Mrs Keiren gives approval, I'm happy to help.'

We run off to find Mr Deery before the bell. He's easy to track down, tending to the school herb garden.

'What did Mr Dinesh say?' he asks when we explain our idea.

'He's totally into it,' I say. 'Just wanted us to run it past you.'

Mr Deery smiles at us. 'I think it's a lovely idea, kids. I'll check with Mrs Keiren, but I'm sure she'll be happy to try anything to mend bridges with the mayor. Come and see me at lunch, and I'll let you know the verdict.'

At lunchtime we get the good news – Operation Plaque Cam is a go! Mrs Keiren wants to see the plaque before it's delivered to the mayor to double-check nothing sneaky's going on, that there are no hidden messages and that it's not going to self-destruct and spray glitter all over the mayor's office, but other than that, she's okay with it.

'Are you sure you can take care of making it, Cookie?' I ask when we're by ourselves again, huddled under a tree in the playground.

'No problem,' she says. 'Dad has a wood lathe and Aaron can do the engraving at the shop. Too easy.'

I don't even know what a 'lathe' is but I'll look it up later. I guess it's an arty thing. Cookie's dad is an artist – a sculptor, to be exact. He has a studio at their home that's always filled with wood and steel and covered in paint. His partner, Aaron, works at a shop in Watto Mall that cuts keys, replaces watch batteries and does engravings. Aaron's also an actor. Not TV, just theatre – the REAL acting, he says, but I've been to the theatre and I'm pretty sure acting is about how well you do it, not *where* you do it. Aaron and Cookie are always going to Balthazar Theatre together to see improv shows (which her dad HATES!). I guess that's why Cookie is super artistic. Some kids are exactly like their parents, I guess. I'm not much like Dad, so I'm probably more like my mum.

'Take this,' says Zeke, handing Cookie a small camera. 'It's an old one that doesn't work properly, but you can use it to figure out how big the compartment needs to be and where to put the hole.'

Cookie grabs it and stuffs it in her pocket. 'Perfect! I'll do it this weekend. It'll be ready to show Mrs Keiren on Monday.'

'That quick?' I ask.

'We don't mess around at the Munsta house,' she says with a wink.

'Can you get it to me on Sunday so I can do the wiring?' asks Zeke.

'No probs. Gotta go!' Cookie jumps up and disappears down the corridor.

'So what are you doing this weekend?' asks Zeke.

'Dunno.'

'Want to hang out?'

I give him a shove with my shoulder. 'You just trying to get away from the madhouse?'

He laughs. 'It's not that mad at the moment. The Tornado has had a good week, and he's crazy cute on his good weeks.'

The Tornado is Zeke's little half-brother, Milo. And Zeke's right. He's crazy cute, but the nickname 'Tornado' suits him perfectly.

Cookie has an older sister who's already at university. I'm an only child. But Zeke? Zeke's family is a different story. Zeke has a brother and a sister. Then his mum married a man who had three kids of his own, and then they had another kid together. That's SEVEN KIDS! How do they even keep track of each other? Our house sometimes feels overfull with just three of us. They have nine in theirs! Sometimes, when I wish I had a brother or sister, I just look over to the McKillop house and think . . . nope, I'm good. There's always something happening at Zeke's house. That's why he likes to come over to mine for a bit of 'time out'. Plus, him and Grandpa get along so well you'd think there wasn't a sixty-year age gap.

'Sure, come over,' I say. 'You can help me come up with payback on Grandpa. He put bubble wrap under the toilet seat this morning. When I sat down half asleep the popping scared the bejeebers out of me. I've got to get him back.'

'Deal. I'll come over on Saturday after I give Mum a hand with the usual morning chaos.'

I can't even imagine what Saturday morning chaos looks like at the McKillop house. I think I'll stick with watching Grandpa make youtiao and then stuffing my face, thanks!

GREEN PEAS RULE 10

DON'T BE AFRAID TO GO ALL THE WAY TO THE TOP.

'It's amazing. How did you . . .?' I roll the plaque over and look at it from all angles. It's sort of like a pyramid but with a flat top. I looked it up and it's called a trapezoidal prism, which to me sounds more like a place to lock up criminal circus performers than a shape. The wood is smooth and shiny and the metal plate on the front gleams. The message is engraved with clean, smooth lines.

PRESENTED TO MAYOR LUPPHOL
FROM THE STUDENTS OF WATTERSON PRIMARY.
THANK YOU FOR 'MOVING WATTERSON
INTO THE FUTURE'.

I almost gag when I read the inscription. If the future is one without Brennan Park, then I don't want to know about it. But Mrs Keiren insisted and I have to think that it's going to be worth it.

'But where's the camera?' I ask, turning the plaque over one more time.

Zeke takes it out of my hands and points to a flowery design carved into the wood below the metal plate. 'It's in there.'

I lean in closer and spot a hole drilled into the centre of the flower. It looks like part of the design. 'That's so cool. You can hardly see it.'

'Correct. Much like a ninja.' Zeke winks at me. I ignore him. He rotates the metal plate to the side and it swings open like a sideways trapdoor. 'And there is the camera.'

Sitting in a little casing is our spy-cam. Honestly, it looks so professional. Like something out of a detective movie. I knew Cookie had skills, but this is next level.

'Seriously impressed, Cookie,' I say.

'Dad and Aaron helped.'

'They didn't get suspicious?'

Cookie shakes her head. 'Nah. I said I wanted the compartment so it could double up as a jewellery box or something, then I did the camera hole myself.'

'And what's that?' I ask, pointing to the black panel below the engraving.

Zeke holds up the power cord running out of the back of the plaque. 'Oh, that's an extra surprise you'll just have to wait and see.'

Usually Zeke's surprises worry me, but I'm so impressed with the plaque I leave it for now. 'Okay, let's go run it past the teachers and deliver it to the mayor after school.'

'Or I could sneak it in there tonight?' says Zeke.

I shake my head. 'Your so-called ninja-ing skills will not be required today, Zeke. Or ever!'

Zeke grins. 'We'll see.'

The teachers LOVED the plaque. Well, to be specific – Mr Dinesh loved the woodwork, Mr Deery loved our initiative and Mrs Keiren loved the fact that it might get her back into the mayor's good books.

So now the three of us are standing outside the town hall, plaque in hand and plan in mind.

The town hall is where the mayor's office is. It's not actually a town hall. Apparently it used to be the school boarding house, way back ages ago before Dad was even a kid. That makes sense because the building looks super old. Like even older than Grandpa, and not much looks older than Grandpa. It has a community space downstairs where they hold meetings, yoga classes and bridge competitions. It's also where Grandpa meets his friends to play Scrabble on Tuesdays, so you can imagine it's a real happening place. Upstairs, there are offices and storerooms full of filing cabinets and papers. On top of that is a clock tower with a big old clock in it. The hall sort of marks the centre of town, with Brennan Park on one side and Watto Mall on the other.

'So how are we going to play this?' asks Cookie.

'I'll do the talking. Cookie, you try to look as innocent as possible. And Zeke, you try not to say anything ridiculous.' I pause. 'You know what, probably best you don't say anything at all.'

'Roger that!' says Zeke. 'Silent but deadly.'

'Just silent will do,' I say, and we walk through the big wooden doors.

Upstairs, in the centre of the reception area, is a big model of our town. But it's not today's Watterson. It's a super fancy, modern, futuristic, who-needs-a-light-rail-in-Watterson Watterson.

Worst of all, the model has a statue of the mayor right in the middle of it. I consider asking Zeke if he has one of his Ninja Turtle figurines on him so we can switch it out, but this is not the time for little attention-grabbing pranks. We've got bigger fish to fry!

The man at the reception desk doesn't look up from his computer so we hover by the model and wait. And wait.

'Ah, excuse me,' I say. The receptionist lets out a big sigh and, painfully slowly, raises his head to look at me. I bite my tongue to stop myself saying something smart. I mean, it's not like a receptionist's job is to welcome and help people who arrive at an office. It's literally IN the job title! RECEPTION – it means to welcome, to greet.

I feel like throwing a dictionary at his head, but I push the comeback down deep and paint a smile on my face.

'Hi there, we're from Watterson Primary and we're here to present a gift to the mayor.'

The receptionist gives another big sigh. My shoulders rise in anger but I hear Zeke whisper, 'Be cool. Be cool.'

'The mayor is a very busy person,' he explains to me at an overly slow pace. 'I don't suppose you have an appointment?'

'No,' I say. 'We don't.'

Another sigh. 'Well, then how about you just leave whatever it is here and I'll make sure she gets it.'

I hug the plaque close to my chest. 'No, that's okay. Our principal wants us to present it directly. Can we make an appointment?'

Sigh number four. He turns back to his computer. As he taps away at the keyboard, another man steps out of an office behind him.

'Geoff, can you send me through the schedule for next week, please?' he asks the receptionist.

Geoff sighs again. 'Sure, anyone else want anything?'

The man behind him rolls his eyes and then looks at us. 'Hey, kids, what are you doing here?'

He seems much friendlier than Mr Sighy McSigh-face at reception, so I decide to give it another go.

'We're here from Watterson Primary with a gift we'd like to present to the mayor to sort of, you know, apologise for the "thing" the other day.'

The man nods. 'Ah yes, the little expression of activism. Have they caught the culprits yet?'

We all shake our heads. 'No, not yet. But Mrs Keiren is definitely on the case.'

'Do you want to show me what you brought?' he says. We walk past the receptionist (who gives us one last sigh for good measure), and I hand over the plaque. 'Wow!' He turns it over in his hands, admiring Cookie's handiwork just like I did. 'This is very impressive.'

I point at Cookie. 'She made it. She's a super talented artist. It's a Cookie Munsta original.'

The man turns to Cookie. 'You're not any relation to Maxwell Munsta, are you?'

'Sure am,' she says with a grin. 'He's my dad!'

'I love his work! I went to his exhibition last year and now I have one of his sculptures in my lounge.' He looks over at the receptionist, who's completely lost interest. 'Do you kids want to see the mayor?'

I nod frantically. 'We'd really love to,' I say, 'We've been told by our principal to deliver this in person.'

He passes the plaque back to me. 'Okay, come with me. Sometimes it's easier to bypass Geoff. He can be a bit of a . . .'

'Sigh-er?' I suggest.

He laughs. 'Exactly! I'm Claudio, by the way.'

'I'm Casey.'

'I'm Cookie.'

We all look at Zeke. He looks to me for permission to speak. *Now* he wants to follow my rules? 'That's Zeke,' I say.

'Nice to meet you all. Follow me.'

Claudio leads us past reception and down the corridor. As he walks, he passes me his business card. 'I'm the mayor's PA. If you ever need anything, my email's on the card.'

'Thanks,' I say, and slide the card into my back pocket. The corridor ends in a large set of wooden double-doors. Claudio stops us just before we reach them. 'Wait here a second.'

He disappears through the doors and returns a couple of minutes later, waving us through. We step inside. My mouth drops open and I instinctively look up at the high roof. The mayor's office is bigger than my entire apartment. It's so grandiose (that's even grander than grand). The walls are made of dark stained wood and lined with paintings and framed photos and certificates. There's a meeting table and some lounge chairs on one side of the room, and bookshelves and large cupboards on the other. A huge desk sits in the middle of it all, facing a fireplace with a large mantle. Zeke nudges me with his elbow and nods his head towards the mantle. He's right – it would be the perfect place for the plaque.

The mayor's on the phone at her desk. She waves one hand in the air as she talks.

'I understand that recycling is important, and I'm sure what you saw was a one-time oversight.

Let me assure you that the recycling is most definitely kept separate and categorically does not end up in landfill. Feel free to head over to my website for more information on all the things I am doing to improve sustainability in Watterson. Thank you, and vote for Lupphol to move Watterson into the future!'

I cringe. Hearing that slogan is like fingernails on a blackboard to me now.

The mayor puts the phone down on the receiver, swivels around on her chair and flashes us an all-teeth smile. 'Children!' she says, raising her arms in the air like she's a long-lost aunt looking for a hug. I feel Cookie recoil next to me.

Mayor Lupphol gets up from her chair and moves towards us, gliding across the floor like she's on rollerblades. For a moment, that dazzling smile wipes all the words from my brain, so I'm super grateful when Claudio steps in. 'Mayor Lupphol, these kids have brought you something from Watterson Primary.'

With the mention of our school, the stride and smile are interrupted for a split second. A look of disgust flashes across her face. It's just a moment, but I see it. Then she's back to the gliding and smiling.

She stops in front of us. 'Oh yes, the school of little activists. Quite a spritely lot, aren't you?'

The glimpse through her mayor-face into the truth behind has allowed the words back into my head.

'Oh, that's just one or two . . . or maybe three bad eggs, Mayor Lupphol. We're not all like that at Watterson Primary. I guess someone was just trying to get some attention.'

Her smile turns into a slight snarl. 'Well, they certainly managed that, didn't they?'

'The rest of Watterson Primary would like to apologise.' I present the plaque to her with outstretched arms. 'In a show of our appreciation and with our sincerest apologies.'

The mayor takes the plaque and reads the message. She smiles and nods. 'Very good,' she says. 'Apology accepted.' She passes the plaque to Claudio. 'Put this on show in reception, and make sure the papers receive a photo of it.'

No! It can't go at reception. We'll never get anything useful out there. I search my brain for an argument but come up empty. I look at Cookie but her wide eyes tell me she's got nothing. As a last resort, I try Zeke. He points a finger at his lips pressed together and shrugs. He always has to take everything to the extreme. 'Speak!' I whisper. He grins and opens his mouth.

'Ah, Mayor Lupphol,' Zeke says, stopping Claudio before he leaves. 'Do you think we could all get a photo together with the plaque in the mayor's office?' He overemphasises 'mayor's office' to make it sound very dramatic and an honour to be there. 'It would make a perfect front page for our school newsletter. The one that goes home to every parent in the school.'

The mayor's lips curl a little at the side. 'What an excellent idea, young man. How about at my desk?'

'No!' says Zeke, stopping everyone in their tracks. 'I think here, around the fireplace. It gives the impression of a warm, yet official setting.'

The mayor nods. 'I like it. If you need a publicity job in the future, give me a call . . . what's your name?'

'Zeke the –'

I give him a look that says, 'DO NOT end that sentence with ninja' and he stops.

' – third. Zeke the third. Long line of Zekes in my family.'

Zeke takes the plaque and places it so it's in the centre of the mantle, facing directly onto the mayor's desk. He spends some time adjusting the placement, pretending he's getting set up for the perfect photo, but I know he's really just making sure we get the best shot.

'And now for the best part,' he says flamboyantly, as he takes the cord and plugs it into a power point above the mantle. The black panel I asked about earlier flickers to life as glowing red letters run across the screen. We all peer closely to read the message . . .

VOTE 1 FOR MAYOR LUPPHOL

The mayor claps her hands together. 'Oh, I love it!' she says. 'Very mod!'

Personally I think it's more than just a little OTT, but I bite my tongue.

The three of us gather around the mayor and Claudio points the camera at us. 'Say cheese!'

Mayor Lupphol puts a cold, bony hand on my shoulder and I do everything I can to force a smile as Claudio takes the photo. 'Okay, this time say, "The Future of Watterson!"'

I think maybe I do a tiny vomit in my mouth as I try to force out the cheesy slogan. All I can think of is Brennan Park and Mum's tree. I manage to stay for a couple of photos, then shiver my way out from under the mayor's hand.

Zeke reaches his arms out like he's presenting a piece of artwork on display. 'Oh, Mayor Lupphol,' he says, waving theatrically. 'See how fantastic the plaque looks here. I think it needs to stay. It matches the wood so well, it highlights the mantle and, let's be honest, the room really was missing a centrepiece. Plus the LED message would be totally lost under those hideous fluoro lights at reception. Wouldn't you agree, Claudio?'

Claudio steps back and takes a look, smiling at Zeke. 'The boy's got taste. He's right, it looks great.'

The mayor shrugs. 'All right, leave it there. Just make sure the papers get the photo and write up a piece stating that if the children of Watterson had a vote, it would be for Lupphol.'

And here comes the vomit again.

Zeke seems to sense that I'm probably not going to be able to contain my disgust much longer and grabs my jumper, tugging on it.

'Well, we'd better be off,' he says. 'Thank you for your time, Mayor Lupphol. Thank you, Claudio.'

'No problem, kids. I'll show you out.' We follow Claudio to the door. I turn to the mayor, but she's already back on the phone, swivelling and waving her hand in the air.

If this woman is in charge of our future – we need serious help.

Trixie Wu's Thoughts On . . .

LEADERS

Just because someone is in a position of power, doesn't make them a leader. A lot of people in this world desire power. A lot desire a better life for themselves. But very few desire a better world for us all.

Trixie

GREEN PEAS RULE 11

FOLLOW *ALL* THE LEADS.

Back in my room, Zeke sets up a laptop on my desk. 'You can watch the video stream here 24/7, or download the footage so you can look back through anything you've missed.'

'Are you sure your mum won't miss the laptop?'

Zeke laughs. 'Have you seen our house? I could lend you ten of them and she wouldn't notice.'

It's true. I haven't been to Zeke's house that many times, but his mum is a total tech geek and the entire place is full of old computers, electronics and parts – it looks like a graveyard in some futuristic land where machines have taken over the world. Zeke gets all his computer skills from his mum because, according to him, his stepdad can barely find the ON button.

Zeke taps away on the keyboard. 'This is a GX5. Mum has so many of these she won't even need parts from it any time soon. It's got a cracked screen and it's missing a 'Z' and a 'Q' from the keyboard, but other than that, I fixed it up to work just fine.'

As Cookie and I watch over his shoulder, Zeke does a bunch of computer-genius stuff and finally an image pops up on the screen. It's Mayor Lupphol's desk! Cookie slaps Zeke on the shoulder. 'Nice work, Ninja-boy!'

I tilt my head. 'Do ninjas use spy-cams hidden inside homemade plaques?'

Cookie grins. 'Twenty-first century ninjas might.'

Zeke looks up at me over his shoulder. I give up.

'Fine! Nice work, but I'm not calling you a ninja.'

Zeke smiles and turns back to our live feed. 'I'll take it.'

The mayor's office is empty but the shot's really great. It's so wide that we can see the entire desk, the cupboard and bookshelves and even part of the meeting table. Unless the mayor's *trying* to hide, there's a good chance we're going to see everything that happens in that office.

'It looks great, but how long will the camera battery last?' I ask. 'We don't want to end up with nothing but three hours of an empty desk while she's at home.'

'Ah!' says Zeke. 'And therein lies the real reason for the LED panel. That power cord is not only powering our "Vote Lupphol" slogan, but also charging the camera. I wired them together. As long as it stays plugged in, we're all good.'

'You really should appreciate him more, Casey,' says Cookie. 'The kid's a mastermind.'

I pretend I didn't hear that. 'And is the sound going to be okay?' I ask.

'It should be,' says Zeke. 'I added a tiny mic to the camera. It won't be perfect, but it should pick up most things. Unless someone's whispering or right on the other side of the room, we should be fine.'

'Awesome!' I say.

'Awesome?' says Cookie. 'Peas, this is the most epic thing we have ever set up. I mean, we're bugging the mayor's office. Green Peas have gone next level here.'

It's true. When I started Green Peas, and began thinking of ways to get people's attention and make them see what was going on around them, I never thought I would end up bugging the mayor's office. But sometimes, when something's really important to you, there's nothing you won't do. I've always cared about the things we have done in the past, I have. I mean, I enjoy the pranks and working with Cookie and, yes, even Zeke, and obviously the cause is important. But when I think about a bulldozer tearing up Mum's park, knocking down her tree, demolishing her bench – I feel a whole new kind of injustice. One so close to my heart that it feels like it's filling up my chest, leaving not much room for anything else.

'New Green Peas rule,' I say. Cookie and Zeke turn to face me. 'We see this one out to the end. Whatever it takes. However much trouble we get into . . .' I look at the photo of Mum on the wall, chained to her big grey ironbark. ' . . . no one is getting rid of Brennan Park. No one.'

'This is an easy one, Casey,' says Cookie. 'Brennan Park is everyone's park. It's not going anywhere.'

Zeke nods. 'Plus, you're our best friend. There's no amount of trouble we wouldn't get in for you.'

I resist the urge to hug him. Sometimes that ninja-kid really has a way with words.

'Even jail?' I ask with a grin.

'Jail, schmail,' says Zeke. 'I'd have us out in ten minutes.'

Cookie raises her eyebrows. 'He probably would, you know.'

And she's right. We sit there for a moment in silence. I'm not sure how I got so lucky to get friends like these. 'You guys are the best,' I say. 'Thank you. For everything. But this plaque-cam is pretty extreme, so let's keep it between us.'

'You're not even going to tell your grandpa?' asks Cookie.

I shake my head. 'Not this time. Green Peas only, okay?'

'Roger!' says Zeke. 'There is one thing I would like to point out, though.'

'What's that?'

'This would be the PERFECT moment for a secret handshake.'

'No secret handshake, Zeke!' I say through gritted teeth and jump up before he can protest. 'Who wants some of Grandpa's pandan cake?'

'I have no idea what that is,' says Cookie. 'But if your grandpa made it, count me in!'

The next week of being a spy is NOTHING like it is in the movies. The mayor's life is *seriously* boring. Meetings about boring stuff. Phone calls about boring stuff. Lots of paperwork which, unsurprisingly, is super boring to watch someone do. Then more boring-stuff meetings. I would've thought running a town was pretty exciting. I would've been VERY wrong!

By the time the weekend rolls back around I can't stand watching the footage by myself anymore, and so on Friday I call in reinforcements.

'Want to come over to mine tomorrow?' I ask Cookie and Zeke as we hang out on the play equipment. Cookie's sitting in the tower sketching and Zeke's making me time him as he tries to beat his own record getting from one end of the equipment to the other with no hands.

'Sure,' says Cookie.

'I'm in,' agrees Zeke.

'Great!' I say. 'I don't think I can handle another night reviewing the mayor's footage without dying of boredom.'

Cookie stops drawing and chews on her pencil for a moment. 'Maybe we need a different approach.' She climbs down to where I'm standing and Zeke jumps off the equipment to join us.

'I'm listening,' I say.

Cookie kicks at the wood chips beneath her feet. 'Well, we can't sit around forever waiting for something to happen. Especially when that might not even be where the shady stuff goes down. What else do we know about her plan?'

Zeke shrugs. 'Nothing really. Except that, according to Casey's grandpa, she's planning on getting rid of Brennan Park.'

'Right, but how do we know that?'

I'm not sure where Cookie's going with this. 'Because she was talking to that lady about it.'

Cookie nods. 'And who's that lady?'

I throw my hands in the air. 'Well, we don't know, do we? We never found out.'

'Exactly!' she says. 'We have another really important piece of information that we haven't even looked into properly. If we find out who the lady is, maybe we can get some insight to their plan.'

Just in case being ridiculously artistic and absurdly cool wasn't enough, now Cookie's having the genius ideas.

'That's kinda brilliant, Cookie,' I say.

She shrugs modestly. 'Well, I wouldn't go that far. But we could try it.'

'Great!' Zeke says. 'I'll do some research online tonight and try to find out who she is. I'll bring any intel over on Saturday.'

'I'll try to get a bit of background from my dad and Aaron too,' says Cookie. 'They know everyone in this town, and everything about them.'

'What about me?' I ask.

Zeke slaps me on the shoulder. 'Lucky you gets to watch the exciting Friday antics of our extremely-boring-yet-possibly-corrupt town mayor.'

I glare at him. 'I can't wait until Saturday when you guys have to sit through it too.'

Zeke rubs his hands together. 'Me neither!'

Cookie picks up her sketchpad and goes back to drawing. 'I can.'

GREEN PEAS RULE 12

Keep your eyes open. You are *always* on the job.

We decide to make Saturday a sleepover. The weather's pretty miserable, so in the afternoon Dad takes us to the movies at Watto Mall. We manage to convince Grandpa to come along, even though he's (as he puts it) 'not a fan of today's excuse for movies'. Grandpa's really into super old black-and-white stuff like Charlie Chaplin and Buster Keaton. But not Dad and I – give us a good Pixar any day. Plus, seeing a movie at the cinema can be a bit of a mission for Grandpa.

We choose a movie with captions, and I ring ahead to make sure that there'll be a CaptiView unit available for our movie. That's a little LED display on a bendy arm that will attach to Grandpa's chair in the cinema. Because he won't be able to hear the movie, all the subtitles will come up on the screen for him. The cinema man assures me there's one available, so we head to Watto Mall.

'Just wait here while I grab my employee ID,' Dad says, as we hover outside the security guard office. Dad gets a discount at the cinema because he's a Watto Mall employee. He takes ages and we're all getting restless. Finally he pops back out again.

'Sorry, I was just chatting to Alil. They got a good clean shot of the guy who's been dumping at the Mall on the security cameras. We need to meet with the cops to try to track him down.'

'Cool!' says Zeke.

'Yes, see!' Dad says to me. 'My job's not entirely boring!'

I ignore him and rush us all to the cinema so we don't miss our session. Dad shouts us with his discount and even gets us a giant box of popcorn. We request a CaptiView device for Grandpa, but the attendant comes back with headphones instead.

'I'm deaf,' says Grandpa. 'Headphones are about as helpful as yelling at me.'

'We need the screen,' I explain. 'With captions.'

Confused, the attendant disappears again and returns fifteen minutes later with the CaptiView unit. We've already missed the start of the movie while waiting for the screen so we grab it and rush in, quickly finding our seats.

I sit next to Dad and kick my shoes off under the chair, tucking my legs up to the side. Saturday afternoons are pretty much the only day-time I get with him, so they're always my favourite. I lift up the armrest between us so I can snuggle in under his arm, and rest the popcorn on his lap so he can share.

About ten minutes into the movie, Grandpa's still fiddling with the CaptiView unit. I lean over to see that the screen just reads 'searching'.

'I've reset it three times already,' he whispers. 'It just keeps searching. Maybe it's looking for its brain?'

I fiddle with the screen, frustrated, but I can't get it to work.

'It's fine, Casey,' Grandpa whispers, patting my hand. 'Just sit back and enjoy the movie.' But I can't enjoy it if Grandpa can't.

I pull the CaptiView unit off the chair. 'We're leaving,' I say to the others, and they follow me out of the theatre.

'This screen doesn't work,' I say, dumping the unit on the counter.

The young attendant looks at me with wide eyes. 'Oh, sorry, I, um, should I get the manager?'

'We'll be needing a refund,' I say, frustrated. 'So get whoever I need to talk to to sort that out.'

After making our complaint and getting our money back, I storm out of the theatre. Grandpa grabs my arm, stopping me. 'Casey, we could have stayed. I don't mind.'

'Well, you should mind,' I say. 'How hard is it to make a simple movie accessible for everyone? It's called open-captions, people!'

Grandpa smirks. 'We'd need to start with open-minded people. It's not that simple.'

'It should be! And if you can't watch the movie, then we don't want to watch it either,' I say.

'Right!' Zeke and Cookie nod enthusiastically.

Grandpa sighs. It's so hard, because I know he doesn't want to 'spoil' it for us, but I don't want to do something that Grandpa can't be a part of. I give him a big squeezy hug that I hope says everything I'm feeling.

'Let's go to Timezone instead,' suggests Zeke. 'Bet I can smash you in a game of *Mario Kart*, Ah Gong.'

Grandpa squeezes me back. 'Challenge accepted, young ninja!'

After a couple of hours of Zeke winning everything at Timezone, Zeke, Cookie and I wait on a bench outside the arcade while Dad and Grandpa go to pee. A massive video screen hovers in front of us, flicking up ads of makeup and furniture and a whole bunch of other things that we should BUY NOW!

'Did you find out anything about our mystery lady?' I ask.

Zeke shakes his head. 'I tried some facial recognition software I've been working on, but I don't think I've got it quite right yet because I just kept getting matches with the *Mona Lisa*, and I can almost guarantee she's not the one plotting with the mayor to destroy our park.'

'Yeah, no luck here either,' says Cookie. 'Dad and Aaron had no idea who she was, but they sure did have a lot to say about the mayor.'

'Oh yeah? Like?'

'Nothing good,' says Cookie. 'They reckon she's all about money and doesn't care about the arts or the community. They said if only someone would run against her, they'd vote for them in a second.'

'Why doesn't your dad run for mayor? Or Aaron?' I ask.

'Because if they actually did something about it, they wouldn't have the time to sit around and moan about it,' Cookie says, rolling her eyes. 'You know what adults are like. All complain, no action.'

It's true. Well, mostly. My mum wasn't like that. She was all action. She stood up for what she believed in and demanded change. Just like I do. I like that we have that in common.

Another ad flicks up on the screen. Futuristic looking apartments with all the 'mod cons', which, from what I can gather, means 'modern conveniences'. They don't look like homes to me. Everything's so white and silver and cold: they remind me of hospital rooms. I wouldn't want to live in one, that's for sure. But, according to the ad, they're an excellent investment and you can 'buy off plan' before they're even built. The camera spins around a giant ugly building as it rises from the ground, built by invisible hands. Text flashes across the screen:

300 X 1–3 BEDROOM APARTMENTS AND
4 X PENTHOUSES. ELITE STAR GROUP,
BUILDING NEAR YOU!

There's something about the blinding flashiness of the ad that leaves me cringing but unable to look away. It reminds me of the video the mayor showed at our school, almost hypnotic. The apartments are being built in Claremont, Mount Aranda and Pambala – towns all around Watterson.

'Ready to go, kids?' Dad says, snapping us out of our video-induced trance.

'Yup,' I say, jumping up. 'Let's go.'

As I turn to leave, something catches my eye. I freeze, grabbing Cookie and Zeke's arms.

'What?' says Cookie. I point at the giant screen. There, next to the Elite Star Group logo, is the smarmy face of our mystery woman, arms folded across her chest in a crisp dark suit.

I read the text below . . .

FIONA GILL. SENIOR PROPERTY MANAGER,
ELITE STAR GROUP.

'Whoa!' says Zeke.

'Mystery solved,' says Cookie.

'C'mon, kids!' yells Dad. 'Haven't you had enough staring at screens for one day?'

We follow him to the car but, truth is, we're going to be jumping straight back on a screen as soon as we get home. I want to find out everything

I can about Fiona Gill and what she wants with *our* Brennan Park.

'Property tycoon Fiona Gill has transformed the town of Pambala with huge apartment complexes popping up in multiple areas throughout the town,' Zeke reads from the article on the laptop in front of us. From what we can gather, Fiona is some bigwig in the property market who reached the top of Elite Star by building luxury apartment blocks in quiet towns that have train access to the city. She then sells the brand new apartments off at prices unaffordable to anybody who actually lives in that town. They sit there – empty, ugly eyesores, blocking out the sunlight – mocking the town that has to look at the big cement buildings every day.

Okay, none of the articles actually said *that*, but that's how I translate it. I can just tell by her narrow eyes, arrogant smirk and crisp steel-grey suit that she doesn't have Watterson's best interests at heart, that's for sure.

'We haven't found anything that actually says she has plans for Watterson,' Cookie points out.

'Yeah, but look around,' I say. 'Claremont, Mount Aranda, Pambala – you don't think we're next?'

'Yeah, it kind of feels like we're being circled by ugly apartment buildings just waiting to make their move onto our territory,' says Zeke.

I flick through the articles on the screen. 'But I don't get it. Why would the mayor destroy Brennan Park just to put up an apartment building we don't even need? I mean, the Grados' house has been for sale for like three months, and no one wants to buy it. At least that has a backyard.'

Cookie tugs at the hem of her t-shirt – today it reads, 'I CANNOT FIT ALL MY CONCERNS ON A T-SHIRT'.

'Look,' she says. 'I don't think we have too much to worry about. Dad says the mayor can't do anything without a majority vote from the council, AND she would have to run any plans past the town first anyway. There's no way the council would agree to getting rid of the park, let alone the rest of the town, right?'

I nod. I mean, adults do some pretty dumb things – like individually wrapping cucumbers and turning on the heater instead of putting on a jumper – but surely they wouldn't get rid of the only park in our town.

'DINNER!' Grandpa yells from downstairs.

Good timing. I feel like I need some food for thought.

After dinner, we check out the plaque-cam. It's a Saturday night, so anyone who worked the weekend has left for the day and the mayor's office is dark. We play back through the footage from the day but once again, it is BORING! I don't know what I want to be when I grow up, but after a week of watching the mayor's every move, I'm pretty sure a career in politics is not for me.

'Can we watch a movie instead?' says Zeke, his chin resting in his hands and eyelids drooping as we watch the mayor go through some kind of checklist with Claudio.

'We only have an hour or so more to get through,' says Cookie.

For once, I agree with Zeke. I'm starting to think our super clever spy-cam plan is less super clever and more super painful. 'Maybe we could just scrub through the next hour?' I suggest. 'See if anyone else shows up? Listen in on any phone calls? And then I'll get Grandpa to do some popcorn and we can pick a movie.'

'*Teenage Mutant Ninja Turtles?*' Zeke asks hopefully. 'The latest one, of course. The CGI is really good, I promise.'

Truth is, I've seen it and it's actually pretty funny, but I've sworn a life-long internal oath **NOT** to encourage Zeke and his ninja obsession, so he'll never know that.

'Not a chance,' I say.

'There's a new documentary about the impending extinction of bees and how it will affect life on Earth as we know it,' suggests Cookie.

I'm all about trying to save our planet, but the last time Cookie chose a documentary for us to watch, it was about the history of logging on

Vancouver Island and I fell asleep in the first five minutes.

'I think *Brave* is a ninety-nine-cent special on iTunes,' I say. I see a look pass between Cookie and Zeke. 'What?'

'Nothing,' says Zeke. '*Brave* sounds good, right, Cookie?'

'Yeah, totally,' she agrees. 'It's been ages since I've seen it.' They both smile at me in a way that makes me feel uneasy.

'What? We don't have to. I know we've seen it a couple of times before. It was just a suggestion.'

Zeke shakes his head at me. 'Nah, it's a good one. Let's do it.'

'Yeah,' says Cookie. '*Brave* it is. Let's zoom through this last hour. I'm ready for some popcorn.'

We get through the last bit of footage super quick. Nothing happens, as usual, and soon everyone in the office packs up and heads home. So we shut down the laptop and head downstairs. While we set up mattresses and sleeping bags on the lounge room floor, Grandpa makes us popcorn, stir fried with sugar and butter. To everybody out there who puts salt on popcorn, I will never understand your thinking. Popcorn with melted sugar and butter is the ONLY way to eat popcorn. We also get wheel crackers and ice pops. I may have grown up in Australia, but Grandpa makes sure I still snack like a Singaporean.

I click through iTunes and find *Brave*. 'Are you guys sure you wanna watch this?' I ask.

'Totally,' says Cookie.

'You bet,' agrees Zeke.

I get Grandpa to put in the code and the movie pops up on our TV screen. I turn to face him. 'Do you want to watch with us, Ah Gong? Should I put on the subtitles?'

Grandpa looks at the movie I've chosen. 'Is this the one about the girl and her mum again? Don't you kids get sick of watching this one over and over?'

'Nope,' says Zeke.

'Never,' says Cookie.

Grandpa looks between them. 'Really? You two like this movie as much as Casey?'

Zeke and Cookie nod vigorously.

Grandpa laughs. 'Those be some good friends you've got there, Casey. Hold onto them.' He waves his hand at us. 'Count me out, thanks. You kids go ahead. I have a crossword calling my name.'

Grandpa settles in at the dining room table and we snuggle down into our makeshift beds.

As the movie plays, I remember why I love it so much. Merida flies across the screen shooting her bow and arrow, fighting for her right to be herself.

I shuffle my face down behind my sleeping bag so Cookie and Zeke can't see my tears when the mum becomes herself again and she and Merida are reunited. Pixar films always tug on the heartstrings but I don't know why this one gets to me the most.

By the time the movie finishes, we're all ready to crash. Grandpa sends us upstairs to brush our teeth and we rearrange our sleeping bags on my bedroom floor.

'Night night,' says Zeke.

'Night,' Cookie and I reply.

Normally we would stay up talking for ages, but I'm thinking about the mama bear and, before I know it, I'm out.

Trixie Wu's Thoughts On . . .

LOVE

It really does make the world go round, Casey. ☺

xMum

GREEN PEAS RULE 13

NEVER TAKE YOUR EYE OFF THE PRIZE.

'Wake up, Casey!' Zeke's voice breaks through my foggy sleep brain. I blink a few times, trying to focus on the redhead in front of me who is all up in my personal space. I finally manage to get him into focus and he grins back at me, stupidly cheery for someone awake this early in the morning.

'She's in the office. On a Sunday. And guess who's with her?'

I try to make sense of what he's saying, with little success. Zeke disappears out of view and I drag myself up on to my elbows. Cookie's glued to the computer screen, Zeke now peering over her shoulder.

'What are you guys doing? It's early. On a Sunday!'

Cookie points to the screen and she's all kinds of serious. 'Casey. Trust me. Get up now.'

That does it for me. The normally super cool, super chill Cookie is anything but. I yank myself ungracefully out of my sleeping bag and peer over Cookie's other shoulder.

There at her desk sits the mayor. She seems to be talking to herself. I rub my sleepy eyes. 'What's she doing in her office on a Sunday?'

'Oh, it gets better,' says Zeke. Just then, another person walks into the shot. Steel-grey suit, pointy features, smug smile.

Fiona Gill.

I feel my eyes regain life and widen like a possum caught in torchlight. This is it. All the boring mayor business we've had to endure is going to be worth it. I grab a chair and drag it in next to Cookie.

'How do you turn up the volume?'

Zeke reaches his arm over towards the keyboard. 'It's just –'

'SHHHHH!' I say. 'Do it silently. Some ninja you are.'

Zeke obeys, quietly tapping the volume button until it's as loud as it goes.

'So what did they say?' the mayor says, leaning back in her office chair.

'At least three hundred apartments,' replies Fiona. 'More if we take over a bit of the Town Square.'

The mayor straightens the pen holder on her desk. 'The park won't be a problem. The town square has a heritage-listed building, but that certainly doesn't make it impossible.'

Fiona sits across from the mayor. 'And what about the council vote?'

'Let's just say I have enough "friends" on the council. I can get anything passed.' When she says the word 'friends', the mayor makes quotation marks in the air using her fingers. 'If you help me keep their pockets lined, our proposals will have no trouble going through on the majority.'

'Excellent,' says Fiona, drumming her fingertips together like a Hollywood supervillain. 'And what about the town? I hear they're a bit sentimental about the park. Especially the homeless lady and her handmade house?'

The mayor leans forward on her desk. 'Who have you been talking to?'

'I never do business in a town without knowing everything about it. And everybody in it.'

'Well, the only person in this town you have to worry about is me. And I can promise you, a nutty town mascot and her silly Lego house are not going to stop this deal.' The mayor leans back again. 'You take care of the costs and let me worry about the people of Watterson.'

'Very well,' says Fiona. 'But you need to get the ball rolling, get the town on board AND make sure you get re-elected to see it through. Can a little old mayor like you handle that kind of pressure?'

Even though the shot is quite wide and the mayor quite small, I'm pretty sure I can see the hairs on the back of her neck bristle. Her back arches, like a cat about to attack, and she pushes back against her desk.

'I've run this town exactly how I've wanted for eight years now. Every proposal I've put through has happened and I keep getting re-elected, so yes, I think I can manage.'

Fiona inspects her fingernails. 'Anyone running against you this year? Or have they already conveniently dropped out of the race?'

I'm glued to the screen like I'm watching an action movie and waiting for something to blow up.

The mayor's nails dig into her desk. 'Don't you worry about my re-election. That will be taken care of. And I'll get council approval. You worry about getting me the plans. My only obligation after that is to inform the town of what is happening, and trust me, Watterson people are only worried about their own day to day. I'll wrap up the proposal in a flashy video and feed it to them with some fancy event. They'll eat it up and, before they even realise what's happening, Brennan Park will be Brennan Luxury Apartments.'

Zeke leans down closer between me and Cookie. 'Do you really think Watterson would just let that happen?'

'Of course not,' I say. But I'm not so sure. See, the thing is, she only has to convince the adults.

And sometimes adults are so caught up with their own lives they find it hard to see the bigger picture. I mean, that's how we got here in the first place, right? The need to be able to take a coffee on the run despite the crazy amount of waste disposable cups make. The desire for the very latest mobile phone, even though the current one could probably last a few more years. It's not that hard to believe that the mayor could convince the adults of Watterson that having three hundred new apartments is more important than having a park. A bench. A tree.

Fiona and the mayor stare at each other across the desk. 'I want to believe you, Mayor Lupphol – that you have this town wrapped around your little finger – but what I saw at that school shows quite the opposite.'

The mayor scoffs. 'That? That's just a few kids with ideas too big for their boots. Don't worry about them. They can't vote. Plus, they've already come grovelling with an apology.' The mayor gestures towards the camera and Fiona spins around. Suddenly, both women are looking right at us. We instinctively duck down to hide.

'Um, guys,' says Cookie. 'You know they can't see us, right?'

Cookie's saying this whilst also hiding beneath the desk, so don't go thinking she's less ridiculous than Zeke and me. We slowly slide back into our seats. Fiona has moved over to the plaque-cam, and she bends in close to read the inscription. Because of the angle of the camera and how close she is, we can see right up her pointy nose and have an excellent view of all the crusty snot clinging to her nose hairs. Not so perfect after all, Ms Gill? Tissue, perhaps?

'Moving Watterson into the future,' she reads. 'I like it. Hook, line and sinker, as they say.' She picks up the plaque, and I feel seasick as the picture swings about the office.

'See,' says the mayor. 'Everything is under control. Now, do you have something for me?'

Fiona reaches into her bag on the floor and pulls out a bundle. The three of us gasp in unison when we see what it is. A huge stack of cash.

'How much do you think that is?' whispers Zeke, as if they might be able to hear us if he speaks any louder.

‘A lot,’ whispers Cookie.

‘A lot, a lot,’ I whisper, knowing how silly it is but not being able to help it.

‘We’ve got them,’ says Zeke, squeezing my shoulder. ‘If we get the mayor taking part in a bribe on video, surely that’s enough to save the park?’

‘For sure,’ says Cookie.

We hold our breaths as we wait for the exchange to take place (and hoping Fiona puts down the plaque before one of us vomits from motion sickness). The mayor gets up from her desk and moves over to Fiona. She reaches out for the money and I feel Zeke’s fingernails dig into my collarbone.

‘Easy enough to convince the council,’ says the mayor, smiling slyly.

‘Looking forward to seeing Watterson “move into the future”. Try not to spend it on a flashy sports car this time,’ Fiona says.

The mayor stiffens. ‘How did you know . . .’

‘Like I said,’ Fiona explains, ‘I know everything: tinted windows and all. Make sure this gets me the permissions I need.’ We hold our breaths as she passes the money with one hand and puts the plaque back down on the mantle with the other. Just before the mayor takes the money, the camera hits the mantle and the screen goes black.

'NOOOOOOOOOOOO!' we all yell at the screen.

'What happened?' I scream, grabbing Zeke by the collar.

'I don't know,' he says. 'She must have put it down too hard and knocked out the transmitter connection.'

'What? How?' I can't believe we just lost the bit of footage that could save Mum's tree. 'How could this happen?' I stare accusingly at Zeke. 'Well?'

'Well, it *is* a homemade spy-cam constructed by an eleven-year-old using his mum's spare electronic parts and mounted in an artistic plaque put together by another eleven-year-old with mad wood-turning skills, so I wouldn't be too ready to give said eleven-year-olds a hard time about a slight failure in the way it functions, considering you contributed very little?' Zeke folds his arms across his chest to emphasise his point. I hate it when he's right. But I'm still super annoyed.

Cookie pushes between us. 'All right, you two, calm down. Less arguing, more problem solving. What do you think happened, Zeke?'

Zeke sticks his tongue out at me and turns to Cookie. 'It's probably still recording. I doubt she could have accidentally pressed the record or power button. My guess is it's just the streaming connection that got knocked loose.'

'Great,' says Cookie. 'So if we get the camera back, the footage will be there.'

'Most likely,' says Zeke.

'Perfect,' I say, with a deliberate huff. 'So all we have to do is get the plaque back. Anyone got any brilliant reasons we could give the mayor as to why we need to take back a gift we gave her only a week ago? Anyone? No?'

A smile creeps onto Zeke's lips. 'Who says we have to tell her anything? Why can't we just take it back?'

'And how are we going to manage that?' asks Cookie.

'Well, we would need someone super talented to make a replica plaque.'

Cookie's eyes narrow. 'I can do that.'

'And then we need someone who is really good at elaborate pranks to cause a distraction.'

I smile proudly. 'Tick!'

'And finally, we need someone to slip into the office and take back the plaque without even being noticed. Someone with certain skills. Say, a covert agent with talents in espionage, deception and surprise who can go undetected in plain sight.'

Cookie grins. 'Are you saying what I think you're saying?'

'That's right, my friends,' says Zeke. 'We're gonna need a ninja.'

An audible groan escapes my mouth, but what choice do I have? I need that camera, and if Zeke's going to put his life on the line to get it back for me, who am I to argue?

'Fine,' I say. 'But please, try not to end up in jail. We'll have no ninjas left to bust you out.'

GREEN PEAS RULE 14

Always listen to others. No idea is too crazy.

The plan is ridiculous. It's more than ridiculous: it's bound to fail. It relies WAY too much on Zeke having some sort of . . . I won't even say it . . . some sort of sneaky skills. I love Zeke, I really do. But the idea that someone as tall and lanky and stand-out as he is can slip by anyone without being noticed is just crazy-talk.

But as well as being ridiculous, Zeke is persistent.

'It's not gonna work,' I say.

'You don't know that,' says Zeke calmly. 'Have faith.'

'How can I have faith in something I know for a fact you cannot do?'

'How could you possibly know FOR A FACT that I cannot do it?'

'Because you are NOT A NINJA, Zeke!'

'But how do you know that?'

Ridiculous. Persistent. And extremely frustrating.

'Because you've never been to Japan. You have zero ninjutsu training. You're not dressed in black. And you stand out like a sore thumb.'

Cookie interjects. 'I've had a sore thumb for a week now and neither of you have noticed. So that saying is pretty ridiculous.'

'See,' says Zeke. 'Even Cookie agrees I could be a ninja.'

'That's not what she said!' I'm almost tearing my hair out at this point.

Cookie plays peacekeeper as usual. 'Look, why don't we give it a go and see. If it works out, Casey, you'll have to admit Zeke's a ninja. If it doesn't work out . . . well, Zeke will probably end up in jail and, let's be honest, I think that's punishment enough.'

'Fine! I give up,' I say, throwing my hands in the air. Truth is, I have enough to worry about with my part of the plan.

'Okay, Wednesday after school then,' says Cookie. 'That gives us three days to get everything organised. All good?'

'Roger!' says Zeke.

'Sure, why not?' I say.

Cookie hands out our to-do lists as the garden shed gives its familiar groan. See, even the shed thinks this is a bad idea! I look at my list. I'm not usually one for bringing attention to myself. I like my pranks to happen anonymously. So the thought of what I have to do makes my stomach twist and I'm not 100 per cent sure I'm up for it. But if Zeke's willing to put his freedom on the line, I have to be up for a bit of humiliation, right? It's pretty elaborate, but we need to cause a big enough diversion for Zeke to switch the plaques, and the task has fallen squarely on my shoulders.

I feel like Cookie got off lightly. All she has to do is make a replica of the plaque – with no hidden camera this time. Although, to be fair, I'd have no chance of doing her job if we swapped lists, and NO ONE has a chance of doing Zeke's. Especially not Zeke. But he's promised if he goes down, he's going to take all the blame, so what can I do? The answer is nothing except get to work on my list.

When I get home that night, I put the first part of the plan into action. I find Claudio's business card and open up my email.

Dear Claudio,

Hi. This is Casey Wu. We met the other day when we came to drop off the school plaque to Mayor Lupphol. The students of Watterson are so impressed with the mayor's dedication to our future that we would love to do a special piece about her in our school newspaper. Every month, we like to do a spotlight on a local hero and we think the mayor would be perfect for next month's issue. We would love to come in on Wednesday after school for a quick interview.

We really hope she can find the time, even though we know she must be very busy.

Kindest regards,

Casey Wu and the Watterson Primary Times

Okay, there's no such thing as the *Watterson Primary Times*. And if there was, I would give it a MUCH better name than that! But I can *absolutely* see myself as a reporter, so it's not that big a stretch.

I read over the email once more and press send. Now to get to work on the second part.

I head down to the kitchen. Grandpa has something bubbling on the stove, but he's in the lounge room hunched over a crossword so I get to work. I grab a saucepan and find a can of vegetable soup. Perfect! I pour half the can in and turn the heat on low. Next, I add a bit of orange juice to thin the soup out, and some milk for colour. I grab two crackers and crumble them into the mix, giving it a stir. It's still a bit thick and doesn't smell quite right, so I pour in some vinegar. Now it's really starting to work.

'What ARE you making?' asks Grandpa, peering over my shoulder into the multi-coloured concoction simmering in the saucepan.

'Oh, just trying a recipe we learnt at school,' I say casually.

Grandpa's nose screws up in disgust. 'Well, I'm glad I take care of the cooking in this house. It looks like vomit!' he says, giving his own soup a stir.

I smile to myself. Mission accomplished!

An email from Claudio is in my inbox first thing the next morning.

Dear Casey,

This is wonderful news. The mayor was very grateful for the lovely gift from you kids. I have managed to block out half an hour at 4 pm on Wednesday afternoon. Is this okay for you?

She has a meeting straight after, so we will have to stick to the schedule, but if there are any questions that don't fit into the timeframe, I'm sure I can help you out.

Look forward to seeing you again.
Regards,
Claudio

I'm ticking things off my to-do list like a champion. Hopefully the others are having the same success.

Zeke's waiting out the front for me when I leave the house. 'Wanna walk to school together?'

'Sure thing,' I say. 'Through the park?'

He nods. 'Might be our last chance.'

I smile. 'Not if we have anything to do with it. And we do.'

We cut through from the back corner and see Cookie coming in from the far side. She's wearing a bright yellow t-shirt and when we meet in the middle I can see it says, 'WITHOUT SCIENCE, THERE'S JUST FICTION'.

'Hey,' she says, waving at us. 'We on track for tomorrow?'

'Yup, I got an email from Claudio – the mayor can see us at 4 pm. My props are ready too. How's the plaque going?'

'Wood's done. Aaron's doing the engraving this afternoon. Zeke?'

'Head-cam is ready to rock. Ninja suit ironed and laid out. I am SO ready.'

He looks so excited that, just for a second, I really hope it works out for him. I know it won't, of course – he'll never pull it off. But the nice person inside me just had a second of hope for him. I know deep down, the next time I see him, it'll be in an orange jumpsuit in jail. I'm not sure orange is going to be Zeke's colour.

'What's Kathy *doing*?' says Cookie, pointing across the park to the Lego house. Kathy's perched in the tree next to the house with a pair of binoculars trained on us. We rush over.

'Kathy, what are you doing up there?' I ask.

'It's a conspiracy,' she says, still staring at me through the lenses. 'They're coming for me.'

'Who?' asks Cookie.

'The government, the FBI, the men in black, the ones in orange.' Kathy waves her hands wildly in the air, almost knocking herself out of the tree. Mr Piddles leaps from her shoulder, finding safety on another branch. Apparently if Kathy's going down, she's going alone.

Zeke reaches up towards the tree. 'Come down, Kathy. Please.'

'Are you with them?' she says, pointing a finger at Zeke. 'You have to tell me if you are. It's the law.'

Zeke shakes his head earnestly. 'I'm not with anybody. Please come down.'

Mr Piddles scampers down the tree and leaps onto Zeke's shoulder. 'See, Mr Piddles trusts me. You can too.'

Kathy hesitates for a moment and finally climbs down. We get her settled on the bench and Mr Piddles curls up on her lap.

'What's going on, Kathy?' asks Cookie. 'What were you doing in the tree?'

'There's people coming here at night,' she says, looking around to check that invisible ears aren't listening in. 'They're measuring and checking and I don't know what else with their little machines . . . maybe reading my mind and stealing my thoughts. You know I've had more trouble remembering song lyrics lately. Maybe THAT'S why!?!?'

'Who are *they*?' I ask.

Kathy shrugs and pats Mr Piddles. 'No idea, but they only come at night. There's one in particular who's running reconnaissance on my home.'

I really want to ask what 'reconnaissance' means, but Kathy looks so stressed out. It's probably not the time. I let her continue.

'An orange-vested evil secret agent with Elvis Presley sideburns. Never trust a man with side-burns, my mum always said.'

I question her gently. 'I'm not sure a secret agent would wear an orange vest, Kathy. They usually go for dark suits and sunglasses.'

'Maybe that's their tactic,' she says, looking at me with wide eyes. 'Hiding in plain sight. It's a thing, you know? But that's not even the worst of it.' Kathy's breathing gets heavier as she strokes Mr Piddles faster and faster.

Zeke puts his arm around Kathy. 'What, Kathy?'

She starts to sniffle. 'They're killing my possums!' With that, she bursts into tears, wailing loudly. Mr Piddles scampers up onto her shoulder and rubs his head under her chin.

This soothes Kathy a little and her wailing turns to quiet sobs.

'What do you mean?' I ask, horrified that someone would even think about hurting such cute creatures. 'Why would anyone want to hurt the possums?'

'I don't know,' Kathy says between sniffles. 'But there's something going on in this park. People creeping around at night, possums disappearing, I even caught someone in my Lego house the other day after I was out collecting rubbish.' Kathy wipes her nose on her sleeve. 'I tell you, someone is up to something. I can smell it.' She sniffs at the air and Mr Piddles does the same.

I give it a sniff too, but to be honest all I can smell is Kathy.

Zeke gives her a squeeze. 'Don't worry, Kathy, we'll look into it, won't we, Casey?'

I nod. 'Absolutely! If someone's hurting animals around here, we'll put a stop to it, you can count on that.'

Kathy's face brightens. 'I knew you Green Peas would be on the case.'

My mouth drops open. 'You . . . you know about us?'

Kathy grins. 'I know everything in this town, kiddo. I love it when kids stop by and tell me about your latest pranks. The last one was the best! I've never liked that Mayor Lupphol. Can't trust her as far as I can throw her. I wish someone would run against her so this town could stay on track instead of hurtling into *The Jetsons* future she has planned for us.'

'What's *The Jetsons*?' Cookie asks.

Kathy sighs. 'Oh, you kids these days just don't watch enough television!'

I can't help but laugh. No adult has said that ever!

'Well, keep us up to date on what's happening around here, and don't you worry, Kathy, we're on the case,' Zeke assures her.

'Wait, does that mean I'm an honorary member of Green Peas?' asks Kathy, sitting up straight in her seat and smoothing down her crumpled jacket. 'I could be your Brennan Park intel.'

I look between Cookie and Zeke and shrug. 'Um, okay, why not?'

'And Mr Piddles too. He's passionately against the depletion of our natural resources!' Mr Piddles cocks his head at me.

'Sure. The more the merrier. But remember, it's a secret organisation. First rule of Green Peas is shhhhhh!'

Zeke turns to me. 'I thought the first rule was, "No acknowledgement of other members during an event".'

'No, we had to change it because you could NEVER follow that rule. It was either that or kick you out.'

'Does that mean I have to redo the rule book?' Cookie asks.

I facepalm myself. Being the leader is a tough gig. 'No new rule book, no new rules. Yes, Kathy, you and Mr Piddles can join the team, just everyone zip their lips about it, okay?'

'Is there a secret handshake?' asks Kathy.

'No! There is no secret handshake!' I groan.

'But there should be,' Zeke says under his breath.

'There's a t-shirt though,' says Cookie.

Kathy claps her hands. 'Oh yay!'

'Which we're never allowed to wear because we're a secret organisation,' explains Zeke.

'Oh,' says Kathy, then shrugs. 'Better than nothing, I guess.'

I can't take any more of this. 'Look, we gotta go. But keep note of what's going on and we'll drop by for updates.'

Kathy salutes me. 'Roger that!'

Zeke smirks.

Oh boy, I've got another one.

GREEN PEAS RULE 15

No Pea left behind.

Wednesday after school, we meet in the garden shed to get organised. Zeke runs through the checklist.

'Replacement plaque?'

'Check!'

Cookie did an awesome job. It looks just like the original.

'Head-cam?'

'Check!'

Zeke has a GoPro strapped to his head like a miner's torch. He has set it up to stream back to my computer just like the plaque-cam. That way we have a record of his moves. Or, as he insists on putting it, his 'awesome ninja skills'.

‘Fake vomit?’

‘Check!’

I tap the side pocket of my bag. I poured my gross mixture into a squirty water bottle. It stinks and looks disgusting. It’s perfect.

‘Whoopee cushion?’

‘Check!’

One of Grandpa’s whoopee cushions is in the other side pocket, already inflated. He won’t miss this one. He has more whoopee cushions than the Hulk has anger management issues.

‘Notepad and camera?’

‘Check!’

Cookie’s decked out like the perfect school news photographer. She’s even wearing a fedora, which suits her annoyingly well. Only Cookie could look so cool in an old-man hat.

‘Ninja outfit?’

Zeke lifts up his school shirt to reveal a black skivvy underneath. ‘Check!’

‘Okay,’ I say. ‘We’re good to go. Remember what we discussed and stick to the plan. That means you, Zeke! No improvising.’

'Me?' he says with mock surprise. 'I always stick to the plan. I AM the plan.'

'Whatever,' I say. 'Just don't mess this up. Keep it simple – distract the mayor, switch the plaque and get out fast. We have one chance to get the camera back and save the park. Let's do it!'

We leave the garden shed and head for the mayor's office.

Geoff, the sighing receptionist, sits at his desk, ignoring us as best he can. The model of Future Watterson sparkles in the sunlight, the centrepiece of the space. The little gold mayor statue in the middle shines brightly, making me want to pluck it from its base and shove it up McSigh's nose so he can never sigh again. Before I finish summoning up the patience to approach the receptionist, Claudio comes sashaying down the hallway.

'Casey, Cookie, Zeke! So good to see you again.'

He's such a nice guy, I almost feel bad for what we're about to do. But only almost.

'The mayor will be out to meet you in just a minute,' he says, showing us to a table next to the town model.

'Um,' I hesitate. 'Aren't we interviewing the mayor in her office?'

Claudio pulls out one of the seats. 'Oh, she's just getting set up for a meeting she has straight after you, so we'll do it out here.'

I shoot Cookie and Zeke a panicked look. How are we going to make the switch if we can't even get into the mayor's office?

'What are we going to do?' I whisper.

'Sorry?' asks Claudio, turning over his shoulder.

Cookie holds the camera up. 'I might just get some snaps for the paper while we wait?'

Claudio nods. 'Just make sure you get my good side,' he says, winking.

Cookie takes photos of the model and the reception area, edging her way towards the mayor's office, Zeke close behind. As they get near, the doors burst open, revealing the perfectly polished mayor. 'Oh, hello, children, lovely to have you back. Please take a seat,' says Mayor

Lupphol, ushering Zeke and Cookie back out to the reception area.

She motions towards the chairs set up at the table. 'Now, I don't have a lot of time, so how about we get straight into it?'

I glance towards the office one last time and then turn to the mayor. 'Ah, we just have a few questions for you and then we'll be out of your way.' I look at my notebook. 'Firstly, we'd love to know what plans you have to make Watterson more eco-friendly and sustainable?'

The mayor shoots Claudio a look. I get the feeling this isn't the kind of question she was hoping for.

'Well, we're looking into lots of different options for how to improve Watterson's recycling systems and waste management. The more we can grow the town and improve its economy, the more money we can justify for these kind of ventures.'

I raise an eyebrow at Cookie. If this was a real interview, we would tear her apart for that answer. But we have to remember why we're here.

Cookie scribbles something on the notepad in front of her and I continue. 'The Watterson

Weeders Society have been petitioning for a community garden for almost two years now. Do you have any idea of when their proposal might go through?'

The mayor grinds her teeth a little. 'The council receives many, many requests on a regular basis and we do our best to work our way through them, but some have to take priority over others.'

'Like the new car park for Watto Mall that you built where the skate park and local businesses used to be?' Cookie's words have a real bite to them that I hope she can keep under control.

Mayor Lupphol raises her chin, looking down at Cookie over her nose. 'Yes. With the Watto Mall extensions we have planned, a new car park was entirely necessary. And the skate park will be relocated once we find an appropriate location and get the plans reapproved.'

I nudge Cookie with my leg. We need to keep the mayor onside for now. This is not the time to grill her and expose her lies. That time is coming.

Cookie lets out a deep breath and writes down the mayor's answer. I push on. 'We'd love you to talk us through what you have planned for our town. Any developments we should know about?'

The mayor's eyes light up. 'Why, I'd love to,' she says, rising from her chair. 'I think you'll be very impressed with my ten-year plan for this town. We will be a business mecca in no time, and you kids will all have jobs thanks to me.'

'But no clean air to breathe,' Cookie mumbles under her breath.

'What was that?' asks the mayor.

I kick Cookie. 'She said that would be something we'd love to see,' I say.

'Excellent. Come over here and I'll show you.' She herds us all over to the centre of the reception area.

Claudio, Zeke, Cookie and I huddle around the town model as Mayor Lupphol takes us through all her planned improvements. I can't help but notice there are no solar panels or community gardens shown – just more buildings, a bigger mall, an extended cinema and an extra factory or two. But Brennan Park is still there, which makes me hopeful that there's still time to save it. Or maybe the mayor's most sinister plans just don't make it onto the town model.

I point to the gold statue in the middle of the park. 'Is that you?' I ask, trying to keep the disdain out of my voice.

The mayor laughs. 'Yes, but of course that's only for the model. The council will vote on who has had the most impact on Watterson and their statue will stand in the middle of the town. I mean, if they vote for it to be me, then that's wonderful.'

The thought of a statue of the woman who's trying to rip down Mum's tree makes me want to vomit. Which, come to think of it, would make what I'm supposed to do next a whole lot simpler. Zeke stares at me with wide eyes and mouths, 'C'mon!'

'Casey,' whispers Cookie. 'Now!'

I reach around to the whoopee cushion and freeze. There are a *lot* of people around. The receptionist, Claudio, a couple in the waiting area, a delivery guy, a woman in a business suit. Is there such a thing as prank-fright?

'Okay,' says the mayor. 'I'm afraid that's about

all I have time for. I have to get to another meeting now.'

Cookie elbows me. 'Now, Casey! Before she leaves.'

I know what I'm supposed to do but the thought of making everybody look at me is too much. I. Just. Can't.

'BraAAAPPPPP!'

Cookie squishes the whoopee cushion on the side of my bag and a sound far louder than I was hoping for comes out. Everyone looks at us.

I freeze, wishing I would just disappear. All eyes are on me.

'Urrrgghhh!'

Wait, that wasn't me. I turn to see Cookie clutching her stomach and bending over groaning.

I put my hand on her back.

She turns to me and whispers, 'You owe me for this!' Then she lets out a second, even louder groan. 'UUUURRRRGGGHHH!'

All eyes are *definitely* now on her.

I am so grateful. I have to make this work. I lean over her. 'Are you okay, Cookie? You don't look so great?'

She groans again. 'My tummy feels bad. I think maybe it was something I ate.'

The mayor looks at her in horror. Sick kids are definitely not part of her schedule. She takes a step back, her nose crumpled up. Claudio rushes over. 'Do you want to sit down, Cookie? Do you need some water?'

Why does he have to be so nice? I need him to move away too. I nudge Cookie. She does a little retch, thrusting her shoulders forward and making a *hurmph* sound. The mayor takes another step back but Claudio remains by our side.

'I think some water is a good idea,' I say, and Claudio rushes off to get it. I turn on the mayor, pointing to a huge framed picture on the wall behind her. 'Mayor Lupphol, is that you with the Prime Minister?' The mayor, happy to be distracted from the sick kid, spins around proudly to face the picture. 'Oh yes, this was last year when she came to visit and –'

'Now or never!' says Cookie. She pulls the water bottle out of the side of my bag and in one quick move she sprays the fake vomit all over the model of Future Watterson, accompanied by very convincing loud heaving sounds that she totally deserves an Oscar for.

'BLUUUUUUURRRGHHHHH!'

'Oh dear,' says the mayor, moving to turn around.

I stop her. 'Don't look directly at it,' I warn, shielding the mayor's eyes from the sight of Cookie's vomit spray so Cookie has time to stow the bottle.

The place erupts into chaos. Claudio runs back in with water, but stops in his tracks when he sees that the planned town swimming pool is now a spew bath. Chunks of carrot and corn cover the roof of the new Watto Mall, and the little mayor statue is dripping in a thick orangey-brown goo.

'Uuurrggh,' says Claudio, trying to hide his disgust. 'Here, take this.' He passes Cookie a plastic cup of water. Normally we'd refuse to use disposable cups, but I'm guessing if Future Watterson's new coat of vomit paint was supposed to have come from Cookie's tummy, then she'd be way too sick to argue. She takes the cup and sits down.

Office staff start to rush around.

'Someone get a mop,' yells one lady.

'I think we're going to need a vacuum,' yells another.

'Everyone just calm down,' yells Claudio, definitely not calmly.

Zeke takes his chance. 'I'm gonna go get Cookie's dad,' he says, but no one notices that he heads off in completely the wrong direction. I watch him out of the corner of my eye until I see him safely slip into the mayor's office. It should only take him a minute to switch the plaque and then we can get out of here.

Suddenly, the mayor clasps her hand to her mouth. Her body lurches a couple of times. 'Are you okay, Mayor Lupphol?' Claudio asks.

'I just can't see . . . vomit makes me . . .' She grabs her stomach and runs off. I watch in horror as she runs towards her office.

'Go to the bathroom,' I yell.

'It's okay,' says Claudio, placing a hand on my shoulder. 'There's a bathroom in her office.'

The mayor grabs the handle, swings her office door open and disappears inside, shutting the door firmly behind her. Shutting herself in. Shutting Zeke in.

Cookie and I exchange looks of terror as we wait for her to come bursting out again, dragging Zeke by his red hair and yelling for someone to call the police. I always knew this would end with Zeke in jail.

Nothing.

'I think we better get you home,' says Claudio.

'I can take her,' I offer. 'Her dad's on his way anyway.'

'Are you sure you're going to be okay?' says Claudio, feeling Cookie's forehead.

Cookie brushes his hand away. 'Yeah, I think it was just something I ate. I feel better now.'

Claudio nods towards the model. 'Yes, well, whatever was making you sick surely isn't in there anymore. That's a lot of . . . stomach content for a little girl.'

Cookie nods. 'Yeah, I'm, er, a big eater.'

Claudio smiles kindly. 'Okay then, off you go, and we'll get this cleaned up. I hope you feel better.'

'Thanks,' I say, actually feeling pretty bad to be leaving Claudio with this mess. 'Sorry about the model.'

'Meh,' says Claudio, shrugging. 'Just between you and me, I never liked it that much anyway.' Claudio winks and turns away to herd all the people back to their jobs.

Cookie and I take one last look towards the door of the mayor's office before we walk outside, leaving Zeke behind, trapped and in trouble.

'He's going to jail! He's actually going to jail. I TOLD YOU he was going to go to jail!'

I've managed to fake being calm until we got out of eyesight of the town hall, but standing in Brennan Park seems like an appropriate time to totally lose it.

Cookie places both hands on my shoulders. 'Stop panicking. Breathe!' she says.

I try to breathe, I do, but mostly I just stick with the panicking. 'And we just left him there. We have to go back.'

Cookie shakes her head and speaks calmly. 'If he'd been caught we would've heard. If we go back, we'll alert them to the fact he's still in there.'

'So what do we do?' I say. 'We can't just do nothing.'

'We go back to your place . . . and we turn on the laptop.'

'The head-cam. Of course! You're a genius, Cookie. Come on!' I grab her jacket and drag her the entire way through Brennan Park and back to my house, not letting go once. I lost one friend today, I'm not losing the other.

The computer takes a painfully long time to turn on, but when it finally does, the screen flickers up in two halves. On the right side, the plaque-cam is black, as expected. I stare with anticipation at the left side, where footage from Zeke's head-cam should be, but it's black as well.

'It's not working!' I say, resorting back to panic mode. 'Or maybe he's been knocked out. Or put in solitary confinement. Or maybe the FBI or the CIA have wrapped him in a carpet and thrown him out of a car somewhere.'

Cookie looks at me like the overreacting fool that I know I'm being, but I just can't help it. 'First of all,' she says, 'I think it's the mafia who roll people up in carpets, not government organisations. Secondly, the FBI and the CIA are both American. Somehow I don't think they'd be concerning themselves with the actions of a Year Six kid in Watterson. And thirdly, look!'

Cookie points to the screen. In the centre of Zeke's black is a thin strip of light. We both lean forward and squint at the screen, trying to make out what it is. The thin strip widens, and through it I can make out the mayor at her desk.

'What the?' I lean back to take in the whole screen again. There are shadows and lines in the black, almost like carvings in wood – it's not actually black, it's just dark.

'Zeke's not in jail!' I yell, making Cookie leap away from the screen. 'He's in a cupboard!'

Sure enough, the thin strip of light is a crack in the cupboard door, visible as Zeke peeks out at the mayor. I look at the time. It's almost five o'clock. So hopefully, if no one's doing overtime, they should all be getting ready to leave soon and Zeke can find his way out.

'What say I grab us some rice crackers and we watch the show?'

'Sure!' says Cookie. 'Can I just call my folks and let them know I'm here?'

'Yup! You can borrow Dad's phone.' As Cookie gets up to leave, I grab her sleeve. 'Hey, Cookie, thanks for today. You really saved me. I never could have pulled off that vomiting prank like you did. You were so convincing.'

She gives me a sly smile. 'All those theatre improv shows of Aaron's must be rubbing off on me. He'd be proud. At least I know if my art career falls through I can always go into acting.'

'I know you're joking,' I say. 'But you totally could. It was a brilliant performance.'

'And the Oscar goes to . . .' Cookie laughs and walks out of my bedroom. Before I follow, I walk over to Mum's recipe card box. I flick through to find the one I'm looking for.

Trixie Wu's Thoughts On . . .

FRIENDS

A good friend will love you even when you make a fool of yourself. A best friend will be right there next to you, making a fool of themselves too.

Trixie

I look over to Zeke's head-cam on the screen. 'You got this, Zeke. Ninja your way out of there.' I put the card back in its place and go downstairs to raid the cupboard.

GREEN PEAS RULE 16

Trust no one. Except other Green Peas, of course.

Dad and Grandpa are in the kitchen. Dad's in his uniform, leaning against the bench drinking his usual pre-work green tea, and Grandpa's cooking what smells like chilli crab. I really want to become a vegetarian like Cookie one day, but I just don't know if I can live without chilli crab. Does that make me a hypocrite? 'Hypocrite' is one of those words that sounds great but actually means something kind of horrible. I want to give up eating all animals, but seafood is my absolute weakness. I really want to try though. I'm giving up one kind of meat each birthday. Last year it was pork, this year it will be prawns. I'm leaving crab until last. I hate that I love crab.

'Dad, can Cookie use your phone to call her parents?'

'Sure,' he says, passing his phone to her.

'Thanks, Mr W.' Cookie disappears into the lounge room.

I tap Grandpa on the shoulder and he spins around. 'Can Cookie stay for dinner please, Ah Gong?'

'Of course,' he says. 'I'll make her some tofu.' Grandpa puts a second, smaller pot on the stove and scoops some of the sauce into it. 'Your dad's missing out tonight, so I hope you're hungry.' Grandpa glares at Dad, who raises his hands in the air.

'It's not my fault you put so much chilli and garlic in your chilli crab that everyone complains when I take it into work. I'll just grab a burger on the way.'

'A burger!' scoffs Grandpa. 'That's not even food. Sometimes I wonder whose son you really are.'

Dad waits until Grandpa turns back to the pot and mumbles. 'Yours, unfortunately.'

I hit him in the arm. 'Not behind his back, Dad. Say it to his face or don't say it at all.'

Dad puts his tea down and rubs his arm. 'Is everyone in this family against me?'

Grandpa dips his spoon into the pot and shovels a spoonful of steaming sauce towards Dad. 'See what you're missing out on!'

Dad slurps it off the spoon and his eyes light up. 'It's amazing. Save me some, okay?'

Grandpa nods, satisfied. 'Okay. But first you have to come over here and help with the crab.'

Dad moves next to Grandpa and starts cracking the crab. I force myself to watch because I'm pretty sure this is the bit that will help me give up crab forever. Plus, I love watching Dad and Grandpa in the kitchen together. I wish it happened more often.

Grandpa adds extra ginger to the sauce. 'Are you going to that meeting on Friday night?'

Dad looks up from the crab with a sigh. 'You know I have to work.'

Grandpa puts his spoon down hard on the kitchen bench. 'Don't you want to have a say in what happens in the very town you live in?'

My ears prick up like a fox. 'What meeting?' I ask.

Dad sighs. 'It's just the regular town info meeting where they go through plans and changes, pretty boring stuff.'

'Boring stuff?' says Grandpa. 'You used to be so involved in this sort of thing and now you don't even care what happens to your own town? Who knows what that shifty mayor has planned. Maybe an airport right next to our house? Would you like planes flying overhead every day?'

Dad sips his tea. 'Somehow I doubt Watterson is getting its own airport anytime soon.'

'Maybe you should go, Dad?' I suggest. 'Maybe we all should. Make sure we're there to stop anything horrible happening.'

Dad puts down his tea. 'Okay, you two have been spending too much time together. There's no big conspiracy afoot, and if the mayor wants something to happen, it's going to happen.

We don't need to be there to protest a new footpath being built. That's why we have a council.'

'You call that bunch of self-important so-and-sos a council? You can't trust them to do the right thing. Everyone knows half of them are in the mayor's pocket.'

'They are? Which ones?' I ask.

Grandpa whips his spoon through the air, spraying chilli sauce across the bench. 'Who knows! That's the problem. No idea who you can trust in this place.'

Grandpa might be more right than he knows. I try Dad again. 'Please, Dad. Can we go?'

'Don't listen to his ranting. This meeting is just another meeting. And, like I said, I have to work.'

'You really should care more,' says Grandpa. 'Trixie cared a lot.'

I can almost see Dad's chest buckle when Grandpa says Mum's name. I bite the inside of my cheek. Dad's hands grip tightly around the hot mug, his knuckles whitening. For a moment I'm scared he's going to throw it at Grandpa.

'I do care,' he says through gritted teeth. 'I care about putting food on the table for this family for the last nine years.'

Suddenly, them being in the kitchen together is not so great. How do they always manage to turn everything into a fight? I face Grandpa, scared of what he's going to say next and hoping it's not something to make the situation worse. But knowing Grandpa, it's almost guaranteed to be exactly that.

"Thanks, Mr W!' Cookie passes Dad's phone to him as she strides back into the kitchen. 'Oooohhhh, that smells great, Mr W Senior.'

Dad and Grandpa let the argument drop, although the tension in the air is almost as thick as the smell of chilli and garlic. Fortunately, Cookie doesn't notice. She sticks her head in the smaller pot.

'Chilli and garlic tofu! Yaaasssss!'

'I've got to get to work,' Dad says. He walks over and kisses me on the forehead. 'Bye, hon. See you, Cookie.' He looks at Grandpa, says nothing, and leaves.

'See ya, Mr W!' Cookie shouts, her head still buried in the pot. I watch Grandpa as he shakes his head after Dad.

'Be back down by 6:30 for dinner,' Grandpa shouts after us as we head back upstairs, our hands crammed full of snacks. 'And don't spoil your dinner with that stuff.'

I'm worried we've missed something during Dad and Grandpa's almost-fight, but when we get back up to the laptop, Zeke's still in the cupboard where we left him. Through the slit, we can see the mayor packing up her desk and getting ready to leave. We munch on rice crackers like they're popcorn at a movie as we stare at the screen, waiting for something to happen.

The mayor finishes at the desk, grabs her brief-case and walks out of view. There's a soft click and the light dims. We wait. Munching. Watching the screen. Munching some more.

The crack widens slowly and the camera moves forward, swinging from left to right as Zeke looks around the room. Because the camera is on Zeke's head, we can't actually see him. It's like playing a first-person video game, but without the controls. Those games sort of make me seasick, so I'm not a big fan of playing them, and this isn't much better. I wish Zeke wouldn't move his head around so much. It's very disorientating . . . if Zeke gets out of this alive, I'll let him know that word came from his book.

Zeke sneaks out of the cupboard and looks around again. The office is definitely empty. He moves over to the main door and cracks it open. The hall outside is empty too, and dark. Everyone has gone home. Zeke shuts the door, turns back to the office and moves over to the mantle. There, in the middle of the screen, is the plaque-cam. He picks it up and swings the metal plaque to the side, revealing the spy-cam and a bunch of wires. He fiddles with a few things that I can't really see – and, to be fair, wouldn't really understand even if I could – and suddenly the second half of the laptop screen flickers to life. It reveals Zeke's face staring into the camera as the plaque-cam starts streaming again.

'Woohoo!' Cookie and I yell, throwing rice crackers into the air.

'What are you two so excited about?' Grandpa's head is sticking through my bedroom door. I didn't even hear him come upstairs. How can he be so loud when I'm trying to sleep and so stealthy when I'm trying to hide stuff from him?

I turn the screen slightly away from him and lean to the side so he can see my lips. 'Oh, just watching, um, a football game on YouTube, Ah Gong. We, ah, just scored.'

Grandpa shakes his head. 'Worst liar ever,' he says. 'Football, really? You haven't watched a game of football in your life.'

He's so right. Why did I say football? 'Um, Scrabble championships?'

Grandpa grins and nods. 'That's more like it. Always make it plausible.' He continues to nod as he leaves. 'Just be down for dinner in twenty minutes, and don't watch anything that's going to scramble your brain.'

Normally, I wouldn't really hide our Green Peas work from Grandpa, but like I said, I think bugging the mayor's office and putting Zeke's life in danger might be a level of rule breaking that Grandpa can't really ignore. Best he doesn't know about this one.

We turn back to Zeke. He finishes adjusting the camera and closes the plaque, holding it up like he's taking a selfie. Now on the laptop screen we have both views – the plaque-cam facing Zeke, and the head-cam showing the plaque. My seasickness just went next level.

Zeke unplugs the plaque-cam and takes the replacement plaque out of his bag. He replaces it on the mantle and plugs it in. The LED screen lights up, but this time with a slightly different message.

VOTE 1 FOR THE PLANET

Zeke looks into the plaque-cam. 'I thought a new plaque needed a new message. Let's see how long it takes her to notice.' He winks into the camera and then goes over to the mayor's desk and starts flicking through some papers.

'What's he doing?' I whisper to Cookie. I don't know why I'm whispering. It's not like I'm the one sneaking around the mayor's office, and Grandpa certainly can't hear me. I think it's the video game effect of the cameras. It really makes me feel like I'm the one doing the snooping, even though I'm safe at home in my bedroom munching rice crackers.

'I dunno,' whispers Cookie. At least she's whispering too. 'Why doesn't he just get out of there?'

Zeke stops searching when he finds a folder full of documents. He goes to the photocopier behind the desk and carefully copies each page.

'Seriously. What *is* he doing?' I ask, but Cookie just shrugs.

Zeke returns the folder to the pile on the desk and puts the copies in his satchel. He holds the plaque-cam up to his face again.

'And these next few are for you, Casey.' He winks into the camera and places it on the desk. Zeke removes something from his bag that looks like a first-aid kit. He puts *that* on the desk too, then opens it up and unpacks it carefully, talking to us at the same time.

'This is a little emergency prank kit I've been working on. I take it everywhere, just waiting for the perfect opportunity and now seems like that very moment.'

The next ten minutes have Cookie and I in stitches. It turns out I've had quite the influence on Zeke . . .

1. First, he takes a small piece of masking tape and tapes over the sensor light on the bottom of the mayor's computer mouse. Classic prank! Now, no matter how much she moves it around, the pointer on the screen won't respond.
2. Then, he heads over to the coffee station behind the mayor's desk and picks up the little jar of sugar. Taking a plastic ziplock bag from the kit, he tips the sugar into it and refills the sugar jar from another bag from his satchel that's labelled 'SALT'. That's gonna be some gross tasting coffee for the mayor tomorrow morning.
3. Next, he places a chair on top of the mayor's desk and climbs onto it so he can reach the ceiling fan just above. He takes a packet of confetti and

carefully sprinkles it along each arm of the fan. The mayor's office will become an instant party when she turns it on!

4. And lastly – and even I think this one is a bit much, but I love it – he raises the mayor's adjustable office chair just a little and then gaffer-tapes an air horn to the chair, just below the seat. If the mayor lowers her seat, it will push the button on top of the air horn and scare the pants off her.

I have to admit, I'm super impressed with Zeke. Not only did he totally pull off the camera switch, but he out-pranked the prank master (that's me!). I've never thought of the confetti one, but I'm adding it to the list for Grandpa payback.

Once he's finished, Zeke quickly runs around the office making sure everything is back in its place.

'Kids! Downstairs for dinner!' Grandpa yells up at us.

Zeke repacks his prank kit and looks into the plaque-cam. He winks at us and grins. 'I told you I was a ninja. See you soon.'

Zeke presses something and the screen goes black. Cookie raises her eyebrows at me. 'You have to give it to him,' she says. 'That was VERY ninja.'

I shut the laptop and follow the delicious smell of Grandpa's cooking downstairs. I don't know if I'll admit he's a ninja, but I'll definitely save Zeke some chilli crab.

GREEN PEAS RULE 17

BAD PEOPLE *MUST* BE STOPPED – WHATEVER IT TAKES.

'It's so good, Ah Gong,' Zeke says, between sucking on the chilli-covered crab leg in his hand. Zeke has always called Grandpa 'Ah Gong' despite the fact the a) he's not even Zeke's grandpa and b) Zeke doesn't actually speak Hokkien, but I know Grandpa likes it. He likes Zeke a lot.

Grandpa looks to me for translation. It's impossible for him to read Zeke's lips with a giant crab leg hanging out of his mouth.

'He said it's delicious,' I explain, and Grandpa smiles, spooning a little more into Zeke's bowl.

Zeke made it back to my house by the time Grandpa was serving up dinner, so of course he stayed. He ducked next door to tell one of his brothers or sisters to tell one of his parents that he'd be eating here, and now he's sitting across from me, stuffing his face when I'm busting to ask him a million questions. Cookie and I have both finished and we're just waiting on Zeke so we can drag him upstairs for a full debrief, but, judging by his appetite, it might be a while.

'Did you kids find out anything more about the mayor's plan for Brennan Park?' Grandpa asks.

We all freeze, the crab leg swinging from Zeke's mouth like the arm on a grandfather clock. I want to say something, but we promised. And you can't break a Green Peas promise – Rule Number 27.

'Um, no, Ah Gong,' I say carefully. 'We hadn't really given it much more thought.'

Grandpa bangs his fist on the table. 'What is wrong with you?' he says angrily. 'I thought you would have been all over this? I thought this was your thing? And the park is something so close to home and you're going to do nothing?'

I'm SO tempted to tell Grandpa what we're up to. He knows about Green Peas, he knows about our other pranks – maybe he would be okay with this. He might even be able to help us. But things are already strained enough between him and Dad – I don't want to add to it.

Grandpa looks so disappointed in me, it hurts. I stare at my plate and move the bits of chilli around with my knife. His voice softens . . . which is even worse than the yelling. 'Casey, that's your mum's tree. And her bench. You're always getting on your high horse about plastic straws and deforestation . . . surely this is even closer to your heart? I'll never understand your generation. You and your father are just the same. Apathy. It's not a very good trait to inherit, Casey. Trixie was a fiery one. She always stood up for what she believed in.'

Grandpa's eyes start to well up. This happens when he talks about Mum. He really loved her, and he remembers her so well. I wish more than anything that I could remember her as well as he does. I want to tell him our plan – tell him I would never let anyone knock down Mum's tree – but now is not the time.

I reach across the table and put my hand on his. 'I do care, Ah Gong. Don't you worry. Mum's tree is not going anywhere.' He gives my hand a squeeze and I put my other hand on top. 'Tell us a Trixie-tale, Ah Gong. It can be one I've already heard – these two wouldn't have.'

I tilt my head towards Zeke and Cookie and they nod furiously.

Grandpa smiles, but that sad sort of smile he does when he talks about Mum.

'It was International Polar Bear Day, years before you were born, Casey-poo, and your mum wanted to join in with the worldwide protests to save the Arctic. So her and a group of her friends dressed as polar bears, laid down in the middle of the town square and poured molasses all over themselves, so it looked like they were covered in oil.'

'Awesome!' says Cookie.

'Yes, awesome until they realised it was going to reach thirty-eight degrees that day, so they were boiling in their bear suits, AND it was way before we destroyed all the bees, so the molasses became a bee and ant magnet. Your poor mum was covered in stings and bites when she got home that night.' Grandpa slaps his knee. 'Ha! Trials and tribulations of an activist.'

'So cool!' I say, imagining Mum rubbing cream on her bites, knowing it was all worth it. I know how she felt. I'd take on a million bee stings to save Mum's tree.

Once upstairs, we sit Zeke in the desk chair and spin him around to face us. If we could have found a couple of super bright lamps to point at him, it would be exactly like a police interrogation – according to the TV shows anyway.

'Okay,' I say sternly. 'Spill EVERYTHING!'

'So while I was in the cupboard, that Fiona lady came into the office.' Zeke leans forward, resting his elbows on his knees like he's telling a ghost story around a campfire. He lowers his voice. I know what he's doing and I don't want to be sucked in, but I just can't help it. Cookie and I lean forward too.

'They talked about how the first problem will be taken care of ASAP.'

'What's the first problem?' asks Cookie.

Zeke shrugs. 'I don't know. They said it's just a "small issue" and that they could blame it on "building code violations" and that "there was no permit to begin with". They didn't seem too worried and talked like whatever it is has already been taken care of.'

'But nothing's happened at the park yet, right?' I ask.

'No,' says Zeke. 'And it won't, *yet*.'

'Why not?'

'Well, there's two things that need to happen before they can move ahead with their plan to build apartments on our park. One – the council vote. And we know how that's gonna go down with the big wad of cash Fiona gave the mayor.'

'Do we have that on video?' Cookie asks. 'Did the plaque-cam catch it?'

'I haven't checked yet, but it was definitely still recording when I got to it – it was just the streaming that got knocked loose, like I said, so fingers crossed.'

'Do we know anyone on the council?' I ask.

Cookie shakes her head. 'I know Dad's been trying to get on it for ages because he thinks the arts aren't getting nearly enough funding in Watterson, but no luck. It's all old people, and friends of the mayor, I guess.'

Zeke nods. 'I looked it up. There's a bunch of people we sort of half know. The son of the police commissioner. Mrs Keiren's sister. I think even one of your dad's bosses from Watto Mall, Casey.'

I chew on the nail of my little finger. 'But we have no way of knowing which ones are being paid off by the mayor and which ones are clean.'

'Nope,' says Cookie. 'We have to be real careful with whoever we decide to take this to. We've all seen on TV how easily this stuff can get swept under the rug if everyone in power is in on it.'

'Exactly!' says Zeke. 'This is big. Like conspiracy-big. And from what I saw tonight, we can't know who to trust.'

'Okay, so it doesn't go past these walls for now. Until we work out who are the goodies and who are the baddies,' I say. 'So what's the second thing? Maybe that's where we can put a stop to it.'

Zeke looks pointedly around my bedroom to add effect. Of course there's no one listening in. Only my David Attenborough poster stares back at him, and I'm pretty sure Sir Dave can be in on this conversation.

'Well,' says Zeke. 'From what I could tell, the mayor HAS to inform the town of any plans to turn public land into private land, or investments or whatever.'

I sit up straight. 'Wait, so the town has to agree to this stupid apartment plan? We're fine then, that's never going to happen.'

Zeke shakes his head. 'No, they don't have to agree. They said there's no vote or anything. The mayor just has to present the plan, like inform the town. That's it. I guess maybe after that if anyone wants to protest or try to stop it, that's another thing.'

I chew a bit harder on my nail. It seems like such a backwards way of going about things. Or maybe it's a cunning way, depending on what your intentions are? It's all so confusing that I'm starting to understand why Dad changed his mind about a political career.

‘So when are they going to do it?’ I ask. ‘At one of those town meeting things that Ah Gong goes to?’

‘No, see, that’s the big plan,’ Zeke explains. ‘They’re going to throw a massive fair in Brennan Park for the whole town. Essentially, they want to distract everyone with fairy floss and rides, and Fiona’s going to put together one of her flashy videos for the mayor to present. She reckons hardly anyone will even pay attention, and those who do won’t really understand that the new apartments mean no more Brennan Park. I mean, we’ve seen those videos, right?’

‘Yeah,’ says Cookie. ‘And she has a point. The way they’re put together makes it looks like Watterson is just magically transformed into a futuristic, sparkly mecca town. It’s not like they show what we lose in the process.’

‘Exactly!’ says Zeke. ‘And that’s their plan. They can officially say they’ve “informed the town” and nobody will even have a clue what we’re in for.’

I turn away, pacing the small space in my room. ‘Well, not if we have anything to do with it,’ I say.

Cookie’s eyes narrow. ‘I can feel a plan brewing.’

I nod slowly. 'It's going to be epic, though,' I explain. 'The biggest event Green Peas have ever pulled off. Are you up for it?'

Zeke and Cookie jump to their feet. 'Of course!'

'Awesome, because we have a lot of work to do. When's this fair planned for, Zeke?'

'In two weeks.'

'Okay, that gives us two weeks to prank an entire fair AND expose the mayor for the dodgy crim that she is. Sound doable?'

'For sure,' says Zeke. 'Especially when you've got a ninja on board.'

I groan. 'You're not a –'

Zeke pulls a pile of papers out of his satchel and waves them in my face.

'What's that?' I ask.

'Just all the plans, vendors and suppliers for the fair including companies and contact details.'

Cookie smirks. 'Nice one, Zeke.'

They both look at me. 'Fine,' I say, snatching the papers out of Zeke's hands and adding them to the Green Peas folder. 'You're a bit of a ninja.'

The next morning, I wake up earlier than usual. I get ready for school, then sit down to watch through some of the plaque-cam footage we missed after the streaming feed stopped. We checked the most important bits last night and we definitely have the mayor on video, clear as day, taking the bribe.

I watch it back one more time. There's zero hesitation as she takes the money. This is not someone who should be in charge of deciding what happens to our town. How does someone like that, someone so corrupt, so greedy, get voted into a position of power? I really don't understand, but I know one thing for sure – I'm going to put a stop to it.

I want to see what else we caught on video after the camera dropped out. I scrub through the footage, stopping every now and then to listen in on a phone conversation or to see who's popping into her office. People come and go throughout the days, but then something catches my eye – an orange vest. At first I'm not sure why, but it's enough for me to stop the video. The camera is pointing at a man's back as he stands at the mayor's desk, talking to her.

'We'll take care of it tomorrow night,' he says. 'The easiest way to get rid of her is to get rid of the house. She'll just move on once it's gone. All vagrants do.'

The mayor puts her hand up to stop the man. 'Listen, Gus, I told Fiona I don't want to know about it. I don't even know why you're here. She's supposed to be taking care of this. Leave me out of it. I don't want anybody even seeing you here.'

'Well, someone has to foot the bill,' says Gus, crossing his arms over his chest. 'And Ms Gill says you're the woman for the job.'

The mayor stands up and slams her fist on the table. 'Ms Gill has already been paid plenty, so I suggest you work it out with her. Get out of my office and don't come back.'

As Gus turns to leave, he faces the plaque-cam, showing some pretty epic sideburns and it hits me – an orange vest and Elvis Presley sideburns!

I check the date and time on the video. It was filmed on Tuesday, which means whatever Mr Gus-Sideburns had planned happened last night. My tummy gives a nervous gurgle as a feeling of dread sets in. Dread and the-morning-after-chilli-crab feeling can be very similar, but today something definitely feels wrong. I run to my room, scribble on a piece of paper and open my bedroom window. I grab for something on my desk and my hand finds a stapler. I think better of it and switch the stapler for an eraser, then throw that at Zeke's window. Nothing. I try a pencil sharpener. If this doesn't work, I'm going to have to use the stapler. A few seconds after the pencil sharpener hits, Zeke comes to the window. I hold up my sign.

BRENNAN PARK NOW! CALL COOKIE. URGENT!

I run downstairs and grab a piece of Grandpa's kaya toast.

'Where are you going in such a hurry? Sit down and eat.' Grandpa points his spatula at the chair.

Knowing he won't be able to read my lips from the kitchen, I quickly sign to him as I run backwards down the corridor. 'Later. Saving the world!'

Zeke comes out of his door just behind me, running to keep up. 'What's going on?'

'Explain when I get there. Did you call Cookie?'

'She's on her way.' Zeke and I bolt to Brennan Park.

As we arrive, my worst fears are confirmed. Kathy sits on Mum's bench, her head in her hands, bawling her eyes out. Her Lego house – gone. I go straight to her and put my arm around her shoulders. 'I'm so sorry, Kathy,' I say, knowing that the words won't help at all.

'What happened?' says Zeke, sitting on the other side. 'Where's your house?'

Kathy looks up, her red cheeks streaked with tears. 'They came last night,' she says between sobs. 'And just . . . they . . . they just . . .' She bursts into tears again, wailing.

Cookie comes running up. 'What's going on?' I point towards where Kathy's Lego house used to be.

'What the?!' says Cookie. 'Where's her –' She stops and bends down in front of Kathy, putting her hands on Kathy's knees.

'It's okay, Kathy, we can rebuild it, I'm sure.'

Kathy continues to sob. 'It's not even the house,'

she manages to get out. 'I loved the house, but it's just a thing. It's . . .' Another wail.

'What is it?' I ask.

Kathy looks at me with red eyes and I can see the pain in them. 'Mr Piddles was inside when they knocked it down.' She explodes into tears again and I almost join her.

'What kind of monster comes in the night and knocks down someone's home?' Zeke asks.

'And murders their best friend?' adds Cookie.

Kathy's sobs get heavier. I don't respond, but I'm pretty sure I know the answer. This is the last straw.

'Green Peas,' I say. 'Meeting. Lunchtime. It's time to put an end to this.'

Zeke and Cookie nod. The mayor has gone too far now. This means war!

'Kathy, do you need somewhere to stay? Can we get someone for you?' I ask.

She shakes her head. 'I'm going to stay here with the possums. The ones that are still here, anyway.'

I nod. Everybody needs their own time to grieve in their own way. I get that.

'What if we come by after school and check on you?' I ask.

Kathy wipes her nose on her sleeve and nods. 'I'd like that,' she says.

'Okay,' I say and give her a hug. 'We're going to find who did this, Kathy, we promise.'

'We sure will,' says Zeke, joining the hug.

'And they won't get away with it,' adds Cookie, piling in on top.

We all stay there, hugging Kathy until her breathing settles. Finally we let her go. I take Kathy's hand and rest it on Mum's brass plaque. 'If you need someone to talk to,' I say, 'Mum's a really good listener.' Kathy nods and I let go of her hand. 'We'll be back.'

We collect our bags and leave Kathy sitting under Mum's tree.

'Someone's definitely trying to clear the park out,' Zeke says, once we're out of earshot.

'And we know who,' says Cookie.

'That's it!' I say, seething. 'Mayor Lupphol is going down!'

GREEN PEAS RULE 18

NEW MEMBERS MUST BE APPROVED BY *ALL* CURRENT MEMBERS.

'THEY DID WHAT!?!?' yells Tess.

Maybe finding Tess Heckleston and telling her about Kathy's Lego house wasn't the best first move. She's been on her best behaviour since the whole 'finding a million bucks in her backyard, spending it and then having a criminal chase after her' thing, but everyone knows she's super fiery. And considering it was her and Toby who organised the building of Kathy's Lego house, I think I might've hit a particularly sore spot.

'Who do they think they are!' Now Tess is yelling at me, and I know she's only in Year Five, but I'm more than a little intimidated. Fortunately, Toby's there too and he seems to know how to handle his best friend.

'Tess, settle down. It's not Casey's fault.' Toby turns to me. 'Do you know what happened exactly, Casey?'

I explain everything to Tess and Toby. What we know about the mayor's plan for Brennan Park and how it looks like getting rid of Kathy and her house is the first step. Toby takes it all in, while Tess looks like she's about to explode. 'I thought I should tell you,' I say nervously. 'Because you guys built it in the first place, and you're so close to Kathy and everything.'

'Thanks, Casey,' says Toby. 'We'll go and see her straight after school. Make sure she's okay. We really appreciate it. Don't we, Tess?'

Tess grits her teeth and nods. 'But I'm still gonna . . .'

Zeke jumps in. 'We have a plan.'

Tess raises her eyebrow and the tension in her jaw disappears just a little. 'What kind of plan?'

Zeke looks to me for approval. I hesitate. Green

Peas has always sort of been *our* thing. I'm not sure I want to share.

Tess sees the look. 'I get it. But maybe we could help? And we're professionals at not blabbing. Right, Toby?'

Toby runs his fingers across his lips, zipping them closed and throwing away the key.

I look at Cookie, who shrugs. 'We *are* going to need help.'

'Okay,' I say to Zeke. 'Go ahead.'

As Zeke explains about the fair and how we want to prank the bejeebers out of it, Tess's eyes light up. When he finishes, she doesn't even hesitate.

'We want in!'

I look to Toby. 'Aren't you two trying to stay out of trouble these days? You know, after your recent run-in with the law?'

'We were,' says Toby. 'Until someone messed with our Kathy. We're on our best behaviour until someone messes with our people. Right, Tess?'

Tess slaps Toby on the back. '100 per cent, Tobes! Count us in. Plus, we have a lot of connections so we might be of some help. Not to blow my own trumpet or anything.'

'All right then, we have a Green Peas meeting at lunch,' I say. 'You should come.'

'Green Peas?' asks Tess.

Suddenly, I feel a bit shy about our secret group. 'Um, yeah, it's the name of our organisation.'

'You guys are an "organisation"?' Tess nods in approval. 'I mean I knew you lot liked to throw the odd prank or two but "organisation" sounds very impressive.'

'Er, it's really just us,' I say, circling my finger between me, Zeke and Cookie.

Toby grins. 'Looks like you have some new members!' He pauses. 'If that's okay?'

All eyes are on me. 'You know what?' I say. 'It *is* okay. I think it's time that Green Peas expanded.'

'Yeah!' agrees Tess. 'And can we bring some friends? With a plan as epic as yours, you might need some numbers.'

Zeke's eyes light up. 'Green Peas goes global!'

'Well, Watterson Primary,' I say. 'We're still a *secret* organisation, remember?'

'Lips are sealed,' says Tess. 'Where do you meet?'

'In the garden shed,' I say.

'That little green one?' asks Tess. I nod and she laughs, shaking her head. 'As I mentioned, Toby and I have connections. You're gonna need a bigger shed!'

Toby turns to Tess. 'Was that a *Jaws* reference?'

She nods. 'Totally!'

'Nice,' he says.

I have no idea what they're on about, but it's good to have them on board.

Tess suggests we move the meeting to the swimming pool change room, and when we get there at lunchtime, I can see why.

There has to be at least fifty kids waiting for us.

'Whoa,' I say, looking around. Kids are sitting on the floor, perched up on the benches and crowded into every corner. They barely all fit in.

'I told you we had connections,' says Tess.

'Yeah, sure,' I agree. 'But this is a LOT of kids.'

'Well, a lot of kids care,' Toby says. 'They care about Kathy. They care about the park. They care about your mum's tree. And they want to do something about it. We know we can't rely on the adults to stop it from happening, so here we are.'

'I also spoke to the other Student Council reps,' says Tess. 'Everyone's on board. You're looking at kids from Years Three through to Six, all awaiting further instructions.'

'Okay then,' I say, and clear my throat. 'First, thank you all for –'

'Stand up on the bench,' shouts one kid.

'Speak up!' yells another.

I nervously step up onto the bench and look out over the sea of kids. My hands start to sweat. Public speaking has never been my thing – I usually prefer a little anonymity. That means I like to keep things secret-squirrel and NOT be the one everyone's looking at.

I clear my throat again. My nerves are ramping up. There's a tug on my shorts.

'Try this,' says Cookie, passing me the sports teacher's megaphone. 'Ms Mezher won't mind, I'm sure.'

I smile gratefully at Cookie and put the megaphone to my mouth. 'Thanks, everyone, for coming.' My voice echoes in the change room. 'So as Tess and Toby probably explained to you, the mayor is planning to get rid of Brennan Park and replace it with some massive apartments that none of us can afford to live in.'

'Booooooo!' yell the kids. I wait for them to quieten down.

'They started the whole thing last night by coming in and bulldozing Kathy's Lego house. And there's some more bad news.'

A murmur spreads throughout the crowd.

'Mr Piddles was inside when it got knocked down.'

'What?'

'No!'

'Not Mr Piddles.'

I can feel the kids around me getting angry.

'We all grew up playing in Brennan Park, and none of us want to see it turned into stinky apartments, right?'

'RIGHT!' shout the kids.

'That park belongs to us. It's Kathy's home. It's our playground. It's the place of my mum's favourite tree. I'm not letting it go without a fight.' I point down to Zeke, Cookie, Tess and Toby. 'WE are not letting it go without a fight, and we'd love your help.'

'Count us in.'

'Just tell us what you need.'

'Anything.'

'Okay,' I say. 'The mayor has a big fair planned in a couple of weeks. It's where she's going to reveal her plans for the park. As many of you know, I like a good prank. So we plan to prank the heck out of her party and expose her for the greedy guts she really is.'

A cheer explodes from the kids around me.

'She plans on sweetening up all the adults with rides and food and fun, so that it's the only thing the voters remember. We need to make sure that doesn't happen. If the fair fails, the mayor fails. And while everyone's in a bad mood about the fair, we hit them with the truth about what she has planned AND how she's doing it.'

'Salt in the fairy floss!' says one kid.

'Slime on the giant slide!'

‘Vaseline to grease up the seats on the merry-go-round.’

‘What if we siphon the port-a-loos into the dunking tank?’

I try to get everyone to settle down. ‘Wait, one at a time. We need to make a plan. It will only work if –’

The kids are getting louder and louder as they talk excitedly between themselves. I feel another tug on my shorts and look down to see Cookie. ‘May I?’ she says, pointing to the bench I’m standing on.

‘Of course.’ I shuffle over and she gets up next to me. Cookie puts her fingers to her lips and whistles so loud I think my eardrums are going to implode. Everyone stops and looks at her.

‘This is only going to work if we’re organised,’ says Cookie. ‘Stop behaving like adults and listen! There’s a big difference between us and them. Our leader cares about the town and about the people.’ Cookie jabs her thumb towards me. ‘So how about we listen to what she has to say.’

The change room falls silent with all eyes on me. I look out at the sea of kids in front of me. Those public-speaking nerves start to crawl their way back into my brain. The megaphone trembles a little in my hand. This is NOT the time to fall apart, Casey Wu! I close my eyes for a second and mentally flick my way through Mum's cards.

Trixie Wu's Thoughts On . . .

FEAR

often the things most worth doing are the scariest things to actually do. You are so much stronger than you think you are. Be brave. Be bold. Be kind. You have it in you.

xMum

My eyes flick open. Mum's right. I have all those things. Her bravery, Grandpa's boldness, Dad's kindness. Cookie puts her hand under the megaphone and gently lifts it towards my mouth. 'You got this,' she whispers, and jumps down off the bench.

She's right – I got this!

'These are the plans for the event the mayor is organising.' I reach down to Zeke and he passes me the folder. 'We're passing around copies of suppliers, caterers and activities. Have a look through it. Tell us if you know ANYONE on this list – maybe a relative or it's your family's business. Secondly, we need ideas on how to prank each and every thing that's going on that day. I've come up with a bunch of ideas already, but we want it to be total chaos so the mayor's team is fully distracted when we carry out the big finale, so we need all hands on deck.'

'But one thing,' yells Toby as he joins me on the bench. 'The pranks have to be good ones. Nothing nasty. Nothing dangerous.'

Tess jumps up too. 'Nothing that's going to cause damage or cost a lot of money.'

Cookie pipes up too. 'Nothing that harms the environment.'

Finally Zeke joins us, and we're so squished on the bench that we can barely move. 'And no animals can be harmed in the making of these pranks. And preferably no people, either.'

'That's right,' I say. 'This is all about POSITIVE pranking. We want clever pranks. Pranks that show the mayor for who she is. We need to know any special skills you might have, and anything you have access to. This is going to be the most epic prank Watterson has ever seen.'

A resounding cheer comes from the crowd in front as fists are punched into the air. 'Cool,' says Tess. 'This is VERY *Mighty Ducks*.'

'Peas fly together?' says Toby. 'Quack, quack, quack, quack!'

I shake my head at them. Tess and Toby have their whole own language that I'm pretty sure I won't ever understand without spending a week glued to the Netflix Cult Movies section.

I continue. 'Toby and Cookie have set up a desk over near the showers. Line up and tell them how you can help out. Once we put a detailed plan together, we'll send out a group email with all the instructions.'

'Ah, Casey,' Zeke interrupts. 'Using the school emails is maybe not such a great idea. Perhaps we should keep this offline? Rule Number 4, and all?'

'Good point, Zeke,' I say.

'I know,' says Tess. 'Let's go old school. We'll do school bag letter drops –'

‘On recycled paper,’ Cookies adds.

‘Of course,’ I agree. ‘So make sure your bag is on your hook. Toby and Cookie, take class details from everyone too.’

Tess nods at Zeke, impressed. ‘Keeping off the grid, nice ninja-thinking, Zeke!’

Zeke beams smugly at me.

We spend the rest of lunchtime getting everyone’s details and organising our crew. There’s a lot of work to be done, so I assign roles and allocate duties. It’s hard to believe I started this. Mum was right, just one person really can make a difference. Especially when that one person is really three. Which then becomes five, and then fifty. I’ve always loved working with Zeke and Cookie, but there’s something super empowering about having so many kids feeling passionate about the same thing you do. It makes you feel strong. Like you matter. Like you *can* change the world.

By the time the bell rings it’s just the five of us left.

'Hey Tess, Toby,' I say, stopping them before they leave. 'Thanks heaps. We really appreciate the help. It would have been a big job for just the three of us.'

Tess laughs. 'I've seen some of the things you guys have pulled off. You would have figured it out. But the point is, it's not just the three of you. What's happening is totally wrong – and if the adults won't do anything about it then, as usual, it's up to us kids.'

'Yeah,' agrees Toby. 'And the thanks is to you, Casey. You started it all. If it wasn't for you, we wouldn't even know what was happening until it was too late.'

'Here,' says Cookie. 'I made these just in case our secret society ever expanded.' She passes Tess and Toby a t-shirt each. There's a pea pod across the front, but instead of holding a row of peas, inside the pod is a little planet Earth. Words underneath read, 'GREEN PEAS – DOING WHATEVER IT TAKES'.

'Now you're officially Green Peas members,' says Zeke.

'Oh, but you can't wear them, because, you know, we're a secret society and all,' I explain.

'Ah, but we can,' says Toby. 'We can wear them under our school shirts. It's very Superman-like!'

The second bell rings.

'We'd better go,' I say.

'Wait,' says Tess. 'Don't you have some kind of secret handshake or something that you all do before you break?'

Zeke and Cookie look at me. I'm starting to get the feeling we should have a handshake.

'Not really,' I say.

'Aw,' says Toby. 'You guys have so much to learn.'

'Hands in!' says Tess. She puts her hand out between us. Toby puts his hand on top, then Zeke, Cookie and me.

'Gooooooo Green Peas!' yells Tess, and we all throw our hands in the air. 'Okay, it needs some work, but you gotta have one.' Tess laughs and heads out into the playground.

I can't wipe the smile off my face as I follow our growing team of Green Peas out of the change rooms. I don't think it needs any work. I think it's perfect.

GREEN PEAS RULE 19

Not everyone will understand what you're trying to do. That doesn't mean you stop.

The next week is a blur of activity. Tasks are assigned, plans put in place and my Green Peas folder is getting thicker and thicker. I'm a little worried how I'll even keep track of it all, but with Cookie, Zeke, Tess and Toby there to help, I feel like it's all relatively under control. I've also discovered something about myself I didn't know. I'm a pretty good leader. Delegation, organisation, inspiration – turns out I'm good at heaps of things ending in 'ation'! Almost every single part of the fair is set up to be pranked. It's the awesome thing about living in a small town – somebody knows everybody.

'Oh, that's my uncle's catering company,' says Costis Nevo from Year Four, at our next meeting. 'Me and my cousin will take care of that one.' He high-fives the kid sitting next to him.

'Great,' I say, scrolling my pen down to the next item on the list. 'A petting zoo has been hired from Zoos2You. Anyone know them?'

The kids look around but no hands shoot up. I look at the invoice details. 'I have a number and an email. Anyone want to take this one on?'

A tall girl at the front puts her hand up. 'I will. I'm not a big fan of petting zoos after a goat ate my cake at my seventh birthday. It would be my pleasure.'

'Perfect!' I say. 'What's your name?'

'Katie Lowe. Year Five.'

I write her name down next to the petting zoo on my list and hand her the paper with the details. 'Do you have something in mind?'

Katie rubs her chin with her hand in contemplation. 'I have some thoughts,' she says with a grin. 'But I do enjoy the element of surprise . . . if that's okay.'

I shrug as she takes the paper. 'Sure, whatever you like. Just make sure no animals get put in danger. I've seen those YouTube videos of when petting zoos go wild!'

Katie nods. 'Animal safety is my number one priority, I promise.'

'Next is . . . the AV stuff. That's you, right, Zeke?'

'Yup, and Mac's gonna help me for the sound equipment.'

Mac Cooper, resident child rock star, flicks his hair and gives me a thumbs-up. He's been very on-board with the plan. I definitely wouldn't describe him as blasé anymore. I'm still working him out, so according to my book of words, he's a bit of an enigma. What's an enigma? Exactly!

Mac leans back in his chair. 'Our manager has secured the band as the entertainment for the fair, which means we'll have access to all the AV equipment.'

'Cool. What's the name of your band again?' I ask.

Toby jumps in. 'We're The Ants Pants. I sing, Mac plays guitar and the Ledden twins are on drums and bass.'

'Perfect. You guys and Zeke work out how we're going to hook our stuff up for the big finale.'

'Roger that!' says Zeke.

Our meetings continue like that – with more and more things being ticked off the list. If we actually pull this off, it's going to be the most extravagant prank-tacular known to humankind.

On Saturday, one week before the fair, Cookie and I spend the day at Zeke's. Most of his family are out on Saturdays. Weekend sports, stuff like that. It's pretty much the only time it's quiet at his house.

We've given ourselves the morning off from plotting and planning to just watch cartoons and hang out. It's nice. It feels like it's been really full on lately, so cartoons are a nice change.

Eventually, after the hundredth episode of *Phineas and Ferb*, I head home for some lunch and to run through the folder one more time. Plus, Dad's not working today, so maybe he, Grandpa and I can go hang out in the park.

As I reach the dining room, I know something's wrong. Dad stands facing me, leaning back against the dining room table, his arms folded across his chest. Grandpa's sort of cowering in the kitchen and won't meet my eye. I stop, glued to the spot on the floor.

'What?' I ask. 'What's wrong?'

Grandpa twists the bottom of his shirt. Dad stares at me. His frown digs the lines on his forehead deeper into his skin. 'Is there something you want to tell me?' he says.

My tummy turns inside out and my thoughts chase each other around in my head. Truth is, there's quite a few things I could be in trouble for, and I have no idea which one it could be. I go with honest but vague.

'What do you mean?' I ask.

Dad steps aside. There on the dining room table is Zeke's laptop – open, with the footage from the mayor's office playing in a window on the screen.

Behind it are all the folders of archived footage, dated and organised . . . and open. I swallow hard. He's found everything.

I am SO busted!

'I . . . I, um . . . I just . . . you see, it's . . .' I've got nothing. What's the use of having a big vocabulary if all the words abandon you when you really need them?

But Dad doesn't have a problem. 'What were you thinking?' he yells. 'You bugged the mayor's office? That's actually illegal! Do you even realise that? She's a respected member of the community, and you're sneaking around invading her privacy when she's just trying to do her job? What has gotten into you, Casey? You were such a good kid.'

This hurts somewhere deep that only Dad seems to be able to reach. Why doesn't he understand what I'm trying to do? Doesn't he see that this is what Mum would do? Why is he taking the mayor's side . . . of ALL people!

'I AM a good kid!' I yell. 'And she shouldn't be a respected member of the community. She's a fraud. Do you know what she has planned?'

Dad throws his hands in the air. 'I don't care what she has planned. It's no excuse for you to behave like a criminal.'

'Well, you should care, Dad. Maybe if you cared a bit more – maybe if you all cared a bit more – she wouldn't be destroying our town. Maybe if you cared a bit, it wouldn't be up to us kids to stop her.'

'Don't be so dramatic, Casey. *She's* not the issue.' He waves his hands towards the laptop. 'This is! What if the police found out? I have no idea how you even did this. I probably don't want to know. I *do* know that this kind of thing takes a lot of work to pull off. You should be focusing that kind of effort on your schoolwork, not running around acting like some kind of radical.'

My fingernails dig into my palms. This is not fair! I'm one of the top kids in my class, and Dad knows it.

'What are you talking about? My grades are great. I never get in trouble at school.'

'Obviously that's only because they don't know what you're up to.' He stops. His jaw tightens and his face turns red. 'Tell me you didn't have anything to do with those other pranks at school. Please, Casey.'

Uh oh.

I don't answer him, but just hang my head a little, avoiding his eyes.

'What were you thinking?' he screams. 'I haven't brought you up to behave like this. You should know better.'

I feel the anger bubbling up inside. 'I do know better,' I growl at him. 'That's why I'm doing something about it.'

'You're just a kid. You don't know the way these things work.'

The anger bubbles over. 'I know exactly how they work,' I say and before I have time to stop it, the words come out. 'Mum would understand.'

Dad hunches forward like I've punched him in the stomach. He holds there for a moment and then straightens. 'Your mother would *not* approve of this, Casey.'

'She would!' I yell. 'She would stand up for what's right. She would do something. She wouldn't just sit around on her butt all night staring at TV screens and listening to podcasts, pretending to protect a mall that nobody's EVER going to rob!'

I know we're just getting each other angrier and that I should walk away, but I don't. And neither does Dad.

'If your mum spent more time worrying about herself and her own health instead of trying to save every single tree and animal, then maybe she'd still be here.'

Dad has angry tears running down his face now. I've never heard him blame Mum before. I've never even heard him say a single angry word about her.

'That's enough now . . .' says Grandpa quietly from the kitchen.

'You stay out of this,' yells Dad. 'You're to blame too, always encouraging her with those silly pranks of yours and your ridiculous stories about being a spy. Did you know about this spy-cam thing? Did you?'

Grandpa looks at me with sad eyes and shakes his head.

'Well, at least that's something! I only have one criminal in the family to deal with.'

'But she's trying to –' Grandpa starts.

'Don't make excuses for her!'

'Don't yell at him!' I step towards Dad. 'Leave Ah Gong out of this. Leave Mum out of this. This is MY decision. If you want to yell at someone, yell at me.'

Dad lowers his voice. 'I don't even want to look at you right now. Get to your room. You're grounded for the next month.'

I ignore Dad and sign to Grandpa in the kitchen – 'I hate him.'

He sighs and signs back – 'You don't mean that.'

Dad steps between us. 'Don't do that in front of me.'

I glare at him. 'Well, maybe you should have come to the course with us. Then you'd understand,' I say. 'Here's a beginner's lesson.' I give him the rude finger.

'Casey!' he yells. 'I don't even know who you are right now. Get to your room NOW!'

I storm upstairs and slam my bedroom door behind me. I'm shaking as I stand at the foot of my bed. I wish Mum were here. She'd understand,

I know she would. She'd be proud of me. I stare at the photos of her on my wall. My anger evaporates and something else takes over. Bursting into tears, I collapse on my bed.

Maybe she wouldn't be proud. Maybe she'd be angry with me too. How would I know? I don't remember her. I don't even know her.

When the knock comes at my door, I don't answer. I'm not speaking to Dad. Now or ever!

'Casey? It's me,' says Grandpa.

I don't even want to talk to Grandpa right now, but there's no point in telling him that through a closed door. I bury my face in my pillow as he enters, half to ignore him and half so he can't see my tears. His weight presses on the bed as he sits next to me.

'Roll over, Casey. You know I can't talk to you like this.'

I give in and roll over. He can see I've been crying and brushes my hair away from my forehead.

'I'll have a talk to him when he calms down. I'll explain things to him.'

I shake my head. 'He won't understand. He'll never understand. All he cares about is going to work, paying bills and making sure I do my homework.'

Grandpa squeezes my shoulder. 'There's more to your dad than that. But yes, he's had to focus on those things . . . to take care of you.'

I shrug his hand off. 'I don't need taking care of. People like Kathy need taking care of. The environment needs taking care of. Brennan Park. This town. Dad just thinks so small. There are bigger problems than whether I've done my maths homework.'

'Not for him,' says Grandpa. 'You are his world, Casey. Everything he does, he does it for you. A lot changed for him when he lost his hearing, when he lost your mum. It hasn't been easy for him, you know.'

I hadn't really thought about it like that. Dad has just always been . . . Dad. Reliable, boring, same-same Dad. I don't know who Dad was before Mum died. Or before he lost his hearing. I always ask Grandpa to tell me Trixie-tales, but maybe I should ask for something else.

'Ah Gong,' I say. 'Could you tell me a Dad-tale? One I don't know. One from before I was born.'

Grandpa smiles. 'I'd love to.' He gets up and goes over to my wall. He points to the photo of Mum and the other students tied to the big grey ironbark in Brennan Park. 'See that photo,' he says.

'Not a Trixie-tale,' I say. 'I know that one.'

'Do you?' asks Grandpa. He points to a student on the edge of the photo. A young Asian man – tall and skinny, with neatly cut hair and a yellow t-shirt. 'Do you know that that there is your dad?'

'Whaaaaaaat?' I leap up from my bed and pin my hands to the wall, one on either side of the photo. I lean in and squint at the figure. It's hard to see my dad in the young man. This man looks defiant and passionate, his mouth open as he yells something . . . but those eyes, I know those eyes. 'It *is* Dad,' I whisper.

Grandpa nods. 'Your dad used to care a lot. He wanted to get into politics and change the world. He was sick of seeing the people in power care just about money. He wanted to help the community and the environment and represent the people.'

I can't stop staring at the photo, but I turn for a second so Grandpa can read my lips. 'What happened?'

Grandpa sighs. 'A few things. First his hearing. It knocked his confidence. Made it hard for him to follow conversations. But your mum really encouraged him after they met. And then . . . well, things changed again after her.'

I look from my mum to my dad in the photo. They made such a great pair – weird and perfect. I always think about the mum I never knew, but now I'm thinking about the dad I never knew. Dad 'before'.

'Ah Gong,' I ask softly. 'Do you think I'm going to go deaf?'

Grandpa shrugs. 'Maybe. It is hereditary. Does that scare you?'

I think about it. 'Not really,' I say. 'If I look at you and Dad, you're both pretty awesome. I mean, I'd probably miss some sounds – you know, like birds and music maybe. But I wouldn't miss screeching tyres or Zeke going on about being a ninja or your trumpet farts!'

Grandpa laughs. 'You'd still be able to smell them though. Sorry.'

I laugh with him and it feels good. 'I'm not scared about not being able to hear. I'm scared about not being heard. The mayor needs to be stopped, Ah Gong, you know that.'

Grandpa nods. 'I also know you spend a lot of time trying to be like your mum. Are you sure that's not what this is about?'

I can feel my cheeks go red. He's right. But he's also wrong. I take his hand. 'I know I've been trying to fight a lot of battles, but this one means the most to me. I have to save Mum's tree and her bench and I have to save our park. Whatever it takes.'

Grandpa smiles. 'You know what?'

'What?'

'Right now, despite having your dad's eyes and hair, right now you look so much like your mum.'

'I wish she was here.'

He puts his hands on my shoulders. 'Me too. But I'm here, Casey-poo. And I'll help you. Count me in!' He pulls me into a hug and I give him a strong squeeze before I pull away so he can see my lips.

'For a deaf guy, you're a really great listener, Ah Gong.'

He kisses my forehead. 'Hearing and listening are very different things. Which is why I don't know why you didn't tell me about all this?'

I drop my head, ashamed. 'I thought maybe I'd taken it a step too far. I didn't want you to get in trouble too.'

'I can take care of myself, Casey. No more secrets, okay? Remember, never lie. Prank, but not lie. Is there anything else I need to know?'

I slowly walk over to my desk and pick up the Green Peas folder. 'I guess you should probably see this.'

'What is it?' he asks.

The idea of confessing to even more of my offences is exhausting.

'Maybe just take a look.'

Grandpa nods. 'I will. And I'll speak to your dad. Until then, try to stay out of trouble?'

Grandpa leaves my room and I go over to Mum's box. I pull out one card I haven't read in a while . . .

Trixie Wu's Thoughts On . . .

YOUR DAD

He is the most wonderful person I have ever met. He's not perfect – neither am I – but we are perfect for each other. You might disagree or fight sometimes, but remember this – nobody will ever love you as much as your dad. Go easy on him, Casey.

xMum

GREEN PEAS RULE 20

NEVER UNDERESTIMATE THE POWER OF POSITIVE PRANKING.

'So it's up to you guys now,' I say to Zeke and Cookie. 'I'll bring you the Green Peas folder tomorrow.'

'But you're the leader here,' says Cookie. 'You have all the answers. I can't even manage to wear the same colour shoes, let alone organise all this. We can't do it without you.'

'Well, you'll have to,' I say. 'Because Kathy still needs our help and the park still needs saving. Me being grounded doesn't change any of that. I'll still do what I can but the reality is, I need you guys to step up.'

This is one of the hardest things I've ever had to do. This is MY prank, MY hard work. But I know there's no way I'm going to be able to run this epic event, or maybe even go to it, with Dad's disapproving eagle eye on me. And the fact is, it still needs to be done. Even if I don't get to be a part of it. It's me who wrote Rule 2 after all. 'It's not about the glory. It's about the message.'

Grandpa took a look at my folder. I was ready for a lecture, but I got the total opposite. Grandpa LOVES the plan. I should have guessed, really. It's got everything he enjoys – pranks, humour, the public humiliation of a person who's abusing their position of power. I should have told him earlier. He promised me he'll talk to Dad once he's 'out of his mood'. Problem with that is, Dad and I have something else in common – we both hold a grudge! Who knows how long it will take him to come around, and we just don't have time to allow for Dad's grumpiness. Zeke and Cookie will have to take charge.

'It won't be the same without you,' says Zeke.

'Geez, Zeke, I'm not dying. It's not that big a deal. Just do it without me.'

But it *is* a big deal. I wanted to be a part of this. Out of everything the Green Peas have done, this one was the most important to me and I wanted to see it through. I feel the tears threatening to return, but I've done enough crying in the last twelve hours. 'Look, I have to go,' I say. 'I'll see you later.'

The next few days are the most miserable of my life. Dad's barely talking to me, so Grandpa's over-talking to make up for it. I feel like I'm slipping out of my own friendship circle at school. I still go to the new, expanded Green Peas meetings, but I've missed so much I just feel like a bystander. Tess has really stepped in to help, and I know I should be grateful but I feel angry at her, jealous maybe. I know it's stupid – she's just trying to help – but she already had her moment (if you can call almost getting arrested for spending a criminal's money 'a moment'). This was supposed to be *my* moment. My chance to make a difference.

On Wednesday afternoon, I walk home alone through Brennan Park. The others are meeting to work on the fair plan, but part of my grounding means I have to come home straight after school. I hear a guitar playing and head for the music. Kathy's sitting in the middle of the park, playing a sad tune on her guitar. I sit down in front of her and just listen quietly until she finishes. She rests her arms on top of the guitar and smiles sadly at me.

'What was that song?' I ask.

'It's called *Seasons In The Sun*, by Terry Jacks. It was Mr Piddles' favourite.'

'There's been no sign of him?'

Kathy shakes her head. 'All the possums have gone too. It doesn't quite feel like home anymore.'

'I know the feeling.'

Kathy lays her guitar on the ground. 'You look like you need to offload, Casey. I'm a great listener. Try me out.'

Looking at her kind face, I decide Dad can wait a bit longer. I start to tell her everything. About the mayor, about our plan, about the fight with Dad – and even about Mum and how much I miss her, and how I'm always worrying I'm not enough like her and wondering if she would be proud of me. It's like turning on a kitchen tap and then not being able to turn it off. It spills out of me, and before I know it I'm in tears – AGAIN!

'What's going on with me?' I say, wiping furiously at my cheeks, embarrassed to be bawling in the middle of a public park.

'Ain't nothing wrong with tears, my dear,' says Kathy, pulling my hands away from my face. 'Better out than in, otherwise you'll drown in them.'

'Sorry about that,' I say. 'Once I started, it just sort of came out.'

Kathy nods. 'Yes, I have that effect on people. I told you I'm a good listener. I'm like the park therapist . . . but I'm free! And the rent on my office is very low.' She winks at me.

'And I'm trying to save your office and I feel like I'm failing. I feel like I'm failing Mum.'

'Come with me, Casey,' says Kathy, standing up and taking my hand. 'I think you're forgetting something. Let's go give you a little reminder.'

She takes me over to Mum's bench, under the big grey ironbark tree, and sits me down. Out of habit, I run my fingers over Mum's plaque.

IN LOVING MEMORY OF TRIXIE WU.

HER FAVOURITE PLACE, HER FAVOURITE TREE,

OUR FAVOURITE PERSON.

'She was good people, your mum,' says Kathy softly.

'You knew her?'

Kathy laughs. 'Honey, I know everyone. I know everyone and all their business. It's kind of my thing.'

I drop my hands into my lap and stare at them for a long time. 'Can I ask you something, Kathy?'

'Of course.'

'Am I like her? My mum?'

'Do *you* think you are?'

I shake my head. 'No. I look exactly like my dad.'

'Sure,' says Kathy. 'But looks aren't everything.'

I think for a moment. 'I don't know if I'm like her. I don't remember her. I don't really know who she was.' When I say it out loud, it hurts somewhere deep down that I can't quite work out.

'Ah, but that's not true at all, Casey,' says Kathy.

She takes my hand and runs my fingers over the plaque again. 'You know what was important to her. You know what she stood for. And she's swirling all around inside of you. That's never going to change.'

'I feel like . . . like I want to make her proud. Even though she's not here.'

'You don't have to be *like* her to make her proud,' says Kathy. 'You just need to be the best version of you.'

'Sometimes I'm not sure I know who I am exactly.'

'And that's okay. You're just a young'un. You're still figuring that out. But you also know what's important to you and you fight for it. I know for a fact that would make your mum very proud.'

'But it's hard, Kathy. No one listens to kids. Maybe we're just wasting our time. Maybe we should leave it to the adults.'

Kathy throws her hands in the air. 'Holy Toledo, don't do that!' she says. 'Nothing will ever happen. Stinkin' adults are the ones who knocked down my Lego house with Mr Piddles in it. Adults are the worst!'

I can't help but laugh. I think sometimes Kathy actually forgets she's an adult.

'Look,' says Kathy. 'It's simple – you have to stand up for what you believe in. Really believe in it, and really stand up. Do something. Make a change. Not for your mum or anyone else, but for you.'

'But it's made Dad really angry,' I explain.

'Well, not everyone is always going to like what you have to say. Doesn't mean you have to stop saying it.'

I lean my head back and look through the leaves of Mum's grey ironbark tree. Kathy's right. I need to stand up for what *I* believe in. Not what I think Mum would. But the good news is, this time, they're the same thing.

'Thanks for the session, Kathy,' I say, closing my eyes for a minute.

'Anytime,' she says. 'I'll send you an invoice later. But for now, I think you've got some visitors.'

Sitting up, I see Dad and Grandpa walking through the park. I look at my watch. I'm only ten minutes late and he's already come looking for me? Dad's taking this whole grounding thing way too seriously. Although I've never been grounded before, so maybe this is how it works.

I really can't handle another lecture right now and they haven't seen me yet, so I leap off Mum's bench and duck behind her tree, out of sight.

Kathy disappears too and Dad and Grandpa take a seat on the bench.

'Why did you bring me here?' I overhear Dad say.

'Because there's something I need to talk to you about, and maybe you'll actually listen if you know Trixie is in on it too,' says Grandpa.

'If it's about Casey, I've already heard what she has to say.'

'Have you?' says Grandpa in an unusually calm voice. 'Because I'm not sure you have. So you're going to hear it again – and a bit more – and this time, you're going to actually listen!'

I peek around the tree to see Dad cross his arms, just like I do when I'm about to get a telling-off. I never really think about Grandpa actually being Dad's dad. I guess all kids get lectures from their parents, even when they're forty!

I kind of want to hear what they have to say, but the idea of listening to my dad getting told off is a bit awkward. Although I have no issue with spying on a corrupt mayor, eavesdropping on Dad and Grandpa makes my gut turn with guilt. I decide to skip it and head home.

As we sit at dinner eating Grandpa's fried Hokkien noodles, there's an awkward silence. Dad has a late start tonight and meals where the three of us actually get to eat together are usually my favourite. But tonight it's just uncomfortable.

I look from Dad, who's staring intensely at his dinner, to Grandpa, who keeps giving me weird smiles. Dad hasn't been speaking to me much lately, so I'm used to that, but now he looks sort of . . . embarrassed or something? After fifteen minutes of this silent weirdness, in which Grandpa makes a few failed attempts at small talk, I've had enough.

'Okay, what's going on?' I say, putting my chopsticks down. Grandpa looks at Dad. Dad looks at

Grandpa. I look at Dad. Grandpa looks at me. Dad looks at his noodles. This is ridiculous.

Finally, Grandpa kicks Dad under the table.

'Ow!' He glares at Grandpa, who nods his head in my direction.

Dad sighs deeply and finally looks at me. 'Your grandpa explained to me about what's going on. At Brennan Park, with the mayor.'

I don't say anything.

Another kick under the table.

Dad grunts. 'I'm sorry I didn't listen to you. I'm still angry at you for the camera thing. Breaking the law, even if it's for a good reason, is still breaking the law, and it won't be tolerated in this house. But . . . if I'd known about the park, about your mum's tree, I would have . . . understood.'

Grandpa looks at me as they wait for my response.

'It's not just about Mum's tree or her bench,' I say. 'Brennan Park belongs to all of us in Watterson. No one's asking us if it's okay to turn our park into a bunch of ugly apartments, and the worst part is, the people in charge are breaking the law to do it.'

Dad nods. 'Why didn't you just tell someone?'

'Like an adult?' I ask.

'Yes.'

'Because they're the ones causing the problem. The mayor's paying off half the council to do whatever she wants just so she can make money. And you know who the council is made up of? Adults! And we can't know which ones are the baddies and which ones aren't.'

Grandpa waves his finger at me. 'She's right, you know! My friend Iman's son is on that council. Even he reckons something shady is going on, because he keeps getting outvoted on everything. And George's daughter is a police officer. Reckons they've been looking into that slimy mayor for a bit now, but no one can prove anything.'

'I can,' I say.

'What do you mean?' says Dad.

I look at Grandpa and he nods.

'Okay, but if I tell you, you can't yell at me.'

Dad frowns at me. 'I can't promise that until you tell me.'

'Fair enough. But you have to at least hear me out,' I say.

'That I can do,' Dad agrees.

And so . . . I spill. Grandpa's wriggling in his seat with excitement but Dad's turning redder and redder as I tell him about catching the mayor taking a bribe on the plaque-cam. When I finally finish, I expect him to explode.

'Are you going to yell at me, Dad?'

He shakes his head, his red face twitching slightly.

I cower a little. 'Are you sure?' I ask. ''Cos you look kinda angry.'

'Oh, I'm angry,' Dad says. 'But not at you. Nothing makes me angrier than dirty politics. We need to go to the police.'

'You can't!' yells Grandpa. 'The police commissioner's son is on the council. We don't know who is involved and what they'll do to cover it up.'

Dad shakes his head. 'I went to school with Ross – there's no way. And his father is helping us find the guy doing the illegal dumping at the Mall. They're good people.'

'Well, you went to uni with Ashana Lupphol too. She was so-called "good people", and look where she's ended up,' says Grandpa.

'We need to let the whole town know the truth,' I say. 'Then it will be out there. And once it's out, it can't be covered up or ignored. Then the town can decide for themselves how they want to handle it.'

'And how do you propose we do that?' asks Dad.

Grandpa stands up from the table and gets my Green Peas folder. He carefully places it on the table and slides it towards Dad.

'What's this?' Dad asks.

'I'm not sure you want to know,' I say quietly.

Grandpa pushes it closer. 'Just the genius work of your incredible daughter,' he says with a smile.

Dad frowns slightly as he picks up the folder. He opens it up and flips through the first few pages. 'Is this what I think it is?'

Grandpa and I nod in unison. We sit there as Dad slowly looks through all our plans for the mayor's fair. Every detail. Every prank. Every protest.

Finally, after what seems like FOREVER, he closes the folder on the table and places his hands on top of it.

I wait.

Nothing.

Just a frown.

'So?' I ask.

'You planned all of this? On your own?'

'Not on my own. With the Green Peas.'

'Green Peas?'

'Yeah. Me, Zeke and Cookie. Plus now Tess and Toby and Kathy and about half of Years Three to Six.'

'And me!' says Grandpa. 'Honorary member.' He smiles at Dad. 'There's room for one more.'

'You get a t-shirt,' I add.

'C'mon, son,' says Grandpa. 'It'll be just like the old days.'

'The old days?' I ask.

'When your dad and I used to prank the neighbours,' Grandpa says with a grin.

My eyes nearly fall out of my head. 'YOU used to prank people, Dad?'

He gives a small smile. 'Just a little,' he says. 'Your grandpa was a bad influence on me.'

Grandpa laughs. 'I told you, the power of pranking is in your blood, Casey-poo!'

Dad picks up my Green Peas folder and waves it at me. 'But it was nothing like this. This is on a completely different level.'

'Isn't it time we did something "next level"?' asks Grandpa.

Dad shakes his head. 'This is big, though. We could get in trouble.'

'We could,' agrees Grandpa.

I nod. 'That's right, we could,' I repeat. 'But we would all be in trouble together.'

'As a family,' says Grandpa.

'And everyone would know the truth,' I add.

Dad drags his chair closer to me and taps his finger on the folder. 'This, Casey, is amazing. How you pulled this all together and rallied all these kids. Not just anyone can do what you've done. And you know the best bit?'

'What?'

'I didn't see anything illegal in there this time!'

I chew on my lip. 'Yeah. I'm sorry about that, Dad. I really am.'

He gives me a squeeze. 'I know you are. But I can see you've thought about this plan. Big impact, no casualties. Your mum would be so proud.'

I squeeze Dad's hand. 'Does that mean . . .?'

'I can't believe I'm saying this,' Dad puts my folder down in the middle of the table. 'But count me in!'

GREEN PEAS RULE 21

If we go down, we go down together.

'Champagne?' I say, running down the list.

'That's us,' say Zara and Sofia. 'We've got our hands on a couple of litres of apple vinegar, should do the trick.'

'Face painting?' says Cookie.

'My sister's the face painter.' A boy in front of me with dark curly hair puts his hand up. I think he's one of the Year Threes. 'I'll take care of that one.'

'Baking competition?' yells Tess.

'Oh, that's me,' I say. 'Well, my grandpa anyway. He's got it covered.'

This is our last swimming pool change room meeting before the big event. It feels so good to be back in the driver's seat. It's exciting and scary all at the same time, but it feels amazing to be part of something. Something big. And with my family behind me now too, I know I can lead this to the end.

'What about the police?' asks Zeke. 'We need the whole town to see, but we especially need the police.'

'I'll take care of that,' says Tess. 'I have, well, let's call it a pre-existing relationship with the police. I'll make sure Senior Detective McKenzie is there.'

'Have we checked if the media's coming?' asks Toby. 'We want to make sure this all gets captured.'

Cookie waves her pen in the air. 'I talked to the mayor's PA, Claudio. You know, checking in as the school photographer. And he says local media will be there. Plus, Zeke and I will be there, covering it all for the school paper.'

'What school paper?' asks Toby.

'Exactly!' says Cookie.

'Okay then,' I say. 'I think we're good to go.'

I close my Green Peas folder and look at the sea of kids in front of me. 'This is the last time we'll all be together before the fair, so I just wanted to say a huge thank you to all of you. I couldn't have done all this without you. And if it all goes wrong, I'll take full responsibility for everything.'

'No way,' says Noah Brizzon from Year Four. 'Me and my sister spent ages researching how to rewire dodgem cars. We want full credit.'

'Yeah! You even said so yourself.' The girl in front of me thrusts a piece of paper with the Green Peas rules on it at me. Zeke made sure everybody got a copy. 'Right here!' she says. 'Rule 21 – "If we go down, we go down together!" We're all Green Peas now!'

The kids start to chant. 'Green Peas. Green Peas. Green Peas.'

Tess leans over and whispers to me. 'This is totally like a scene from a movie. We should have some theme music, you know?'

I shrug. I'm no movie or music expert but one thing I do know is that this is super cool.

When the big day finally arrives, it's kind of weird. I don't actually have that much to do. I feel like some grand chess master who's put all the pieces into place, and now just has to watch their opponent stumble their way into checkmate.

I take Mum's tree photo and give her a kiss. 'Wish me luck, Mum.' I pick up the card I laid out for myself last night.

Trixie Wu's Thoughts On . . .

PERSISTENCE

The most rewarding things are never easy to achieve, Casey. The more important something is, the harder you have to work at it. But keep at it, because when you finally get there, nothing will feel as good. Never let anyone tell you 'you can't'.

xMum

'Casey!' yells Dad. 'You almost ready?'

I run downstairs. Dad's waiting in the kitchen, and Grandpa's packing us some food. By the looks of it, he's packing food for the entire town.

I touch his arm and he turns to face me. 'That's a lot of food, Ah Gong.'

'Well, I've read through that folder of yours and my spidey-sense tells me we probably don't want to be eating from the food vans at the fair, right?' He winks at me.

'Good point!' I join him in the kitchen. 'Can you pack extra for Kathy too, please? Your yummy cooking might help cheer her up.'

Dad stuffs his jumper into a backpack. 'Why does Kathy need cheering up?'

I turn to him, confused. 'I didn't tell you about her house?'

Dad shakes his head.

'Her Lego house got knocked down in the middle of the night by one of Mayor Lupphol's cronies. Some orange-vested creep called Gus with Elvis Presley sideburns. And if I find out who he is, I'm going to give him a piece of my mind.'

Dad stops, his jumper hanging half out of his bag. 'Did you say sideburns?'

'Yeah. Huge, furry dark ones. Ridiculous.'

'What did you say his name was?'

'Gus-something.'

'What kind of car does he drive?'

'How would I know?' I stare at my frozen Dad. 'What? What is it?'

Dad snaps out of it and turns to Grandpa. 'Can you take Casey to the fair? I'll meet you both there.'

'Sure,' says Grandpa. 'But why?'

Dad grabs his bag and rushes out the door. 'I have to check something . . .'

'But Dad!' I yell. It's too late, he's already gone. 'What was that all about?' I ask Grandpa, but he's not looking at me so I just leave it.

When we arrive in Brennan Park, everything's set up. The fairground has been fenced off, and there's a line of people from the front gate all the way down the side of the park. Inside the fence is everything we expected to see – rides, stalls, food vans, tents and a big stage with a giant video screen – the mayor has definitely gone all out. Grandpa and

I walk down the row of people and join the end of the line.

'I can't believe how excited the kids are about this fair,' says one of the parents in line. 'Normally they'd think it's "lame" and I'd have to drag them here kicking and screaming.' The kid in line, who I think is in Year Three, winks at me.

'Mine too,' says another parent. 'They even made me come early so they wouldn't miss anything. What they thought they were going to miss is beyond me. Usually pony rides and face painting is not their thing. But not today.'

I smile.

'What are you grinning about?' says Grandpa. 'Other than the obvious?'

I just mouth the words so the parents can't hear me, but Grandpa can still understand. 'There's a bit of buzz about the fair apparently.'

Grandpa nods and squeezes my hand.

A bunch more people have joined the line now, and something's happening down the end. I stand on my tippy-toes to see the mayor has arrived. She's making her way down the line, followed by a camera crew who are filming her every move. Perfect!

'Thank you for coming, you're going to have a wonderful time,' she says to the people, shaking their hands. 'Don't forget to get your free glass of champagne on arrival, and you kids have to try the fairy floss. Also, "Vote for Lupphol" showbags are available for everyone.'

She pats kids on the head, who glare at her as she moves down the line – she's still talking, but not to anyone in particular. 'Yes, it was all organised by me, doing what I can for the people of Watterson. I care about you and what you want. Make sure you see the petting zoo and try a cake at the bake-off.'

A photographer follows her as well as the TV crew. She stops next to a man holding his baby. 'What a cute baby! How about we get a photo?'

'Sure,' says the man, who's struggling with bags, a pram and two other small kids. 'Want to hold him?'

The mayor shrinks back from the baby like he has fleas or something. 'No, no, that's fine,' she says. 'You hold it. I'll just stand here. Now smile!'

The mayor pastes a perfect full-teeth smile across her face, waits for the flash and then moves quickly away before she catches the baby-fleas.

She reaches Grandpa and I. 'Lovely to see our elderly citizens joining in the fun,' she says.

'I'm not THAT old,' snaps Grandpa. I elbow him and he forces a smile. 'Not too old for a bit of fun, that is.'

'Right, yes, very good,' says the mayor and turns to me. 'Oh, if it isn't our little reporter. You didn't bring your seasick assistant, did you?' She takes a step away from me. I think she's worried I've caught Cookie's bug and is wary of my imminent projectile vomit potential, even two weeks later. 'No spinning rides for you today, young lady!'

I force a smile on my face. 'No, Mayor Lupphol,' I say. 'But I don't think it's me you should be worried about.'

The mayor's brow creases but she moves on, continuing her way down the line. When she finally reaches the gate, she takes a megaphone.

'Welcome, people of Watterson, to this town fair, organised by yours truly as a celebration of how far I have brought this town, and how far into the future I intend for us to go. I have big plans for Watterson, some of which you will see later today.' The TV crew hover close by, filming her every word while the photographer snaps away. 'But for now, just relax, have fun, indulge and enjoy yourself knowing your town is in safe hands with me. And remember, vote one for Mayor Lupphol in the upcoming election. I declare the town fair OPEN!'

The gates fly open and the people of Watterson begin to shuffle in. Kids spread out in all directions as their parents yell after them to stay with their siblings and keep out of trouble.

I watch as the mayor tosses the megaphone to an assistant. 'Hand sanitiser! Hand sanitiser, people. Now!' Someone squeezes some gel into her cupped hands and she rubs them together, trying to get rid of all the 'people-germs'.

Grandpa and I make our way through the gates. He pats me on the back. 'Okay then, off you go.'

I grin at him. 'Aren't you going to tell me to stay out of trouble?'

He shakes his head and leans down, looking in my eyes. 'Casey, go get in as much trouble as you can. I'm sorry I doubted that you cared. I should have known better. It's incredible what you've organised. Pranking at its best. I have a feeling this is going to be the proudest day of my life.' I give him a kiss on the cheek, then run off to find Zeke and Cookie.

They're over at the coffee stand, where Cookie's dad and Aaron are chatting to Zeke's mum. Zeke's brothers and sisters are scattered around, the smaller ones dragging on the limbs of the older ones.

'What say we go check this place out?' I ask.

'Please!' says Zeke, as his younger brother yanks on the back pocket of his jeans.

'Parentals!' yells Cookie. 'We're going to check things out, okay?'

'Sure, just stay together,' says Cookie's dad.

'And meet at the stage like we planned,' adds Aaron.

'Same for you, Zeke!' calls his mum. 'Are you taking your brother?'

'Can't, sorry,' says Zeke. 'We gotta do stuff for school.' Zeke peels his brother off his leg and passes him back to his mum.

'Hi, Casey,' says Zeke's mum, smiling at me. She has such a nice smile.

'Hi,' I say, giving a quick wave, and the three of us run off.

'Claudio's expecting us,' explains Cookie. 'I told him we're covering the fair for the school newspaper, so we're going to follow the mayor around. It'll give us a front-row seat to the action.' Cookie holds up her camera and winks.

'And I brought this.' Zeke holds up a GoPro on a stick that sort of suspends it in the air as he moves around. 'That way we'll get it all on film too.'

'Does your mum ever care that you just swipe all her stuff?' I ask.

'Not when it's for something as respectful as a school project.'

'What did you tell your dad?' Cookie asks.

I pause. 'The truth.'

'Whaaaaaat?' Cookie and Zeke stare at me like I've gone crazy.

I shrug. 'I told him what was happening and about the mayor and Mum's tree and how we didn't know who we could trust and it was up to us – and he actually listened. I explained that we're all about *positive* pranking, exposing the truth and he got it, you know. Not only did he get it, actually, he's on board. Grandpa too.'

'*Whoa!* Your dad is so cool,' says Cookie.

'Soooooo cool,' agrees Zeke.

I smile. 'You know what? He is, isn't he?' I make a mental note to give Dad a hug later. 'C'mon, let's go find the mayor.'

It's not hard to find her, given her entourage. It's like a school of fish moving around the fair.

We squeeze our way in and I give Claudio a little wave, who smiles back. He continues to explain the plan to the group.

'We'll move the mayor around the fair and get some good shots of her with the locals – sharing a champagne, tasting something at the baking competition, patting the animals, playing with the kids, that kind of thing. Try to always get her doing everything with a member of the community.

Then, once we've ticked off each of the events, we'll move to the main stage. The band will play the mayor's chosen intro song, which is . . .' Claudio flicks through the pages on his clipboard and chews on his lip. 'Um . . . "Simply The Best" by Tina Turner, and the mayor will be introduced by a local supporter . . . Have we confirmed who this is yet?'

A young woman standing next to Claudio flicks over a page on her own clipboard and runs her pen down the list. She looks up and shakes her head.

Claudio sighs. 'Confirm it for us NOW! Get a business owner or a teacher – someone the town likes and respects. Then the mayor will come on stage, give a short speech and we play the video. Who's on the video?'

The young woman raises her hand. 'I've given the file to the AV people and it's ready to go.'

'Great, but I want one of us there too. Jess, can you handle that?'

Jess nods nervously. She doesn't look entirely sure she *can* handle it – which will work out great for us.

'All right' says Claudio. 'Everyone ready? Mayor Lupphol?'

The mayor nods and straightens her jacket.

Claudio claps his hands. 'Let's go mingle with the public.'

I catch a grimace on the mayor's face as she follows Claudio towards the drinks tent. She looks like she'd rather lick cat's fur than mingle with us mere mortals. Which makes today just more and more perfect.

I scan the crowd at the fair. Kids are everywhere, playing and laughing, but it's all a façade. (I love words with accents on them – they're like superspy words from other languages that have snuck their way into English but refuse to conform.) Behind the fake smiles and robotic play, kids are watching, waiting, prepared. Every kid, every Green Pea, knows – the time for action is now.

GREEN PEAS RULE 22

When the going gets tough, the tough get pranking.

First stop is the drinks tent. Zara and Sofia hover nearby, hands behind their backs, looking as innocent as possible. Claudio gathers everyone and passes around welcome champagne to all the adults. Someone else hands out lemonade for us kids. I check the lemonade for a second, a little worried, but when I look up, the girls give me the thumbs-up to assure me it's A-okay.

The mayor raises her glass into the air. 'To celebrate this wonderful day, and all that I have given to the town of Watterson, let us share in a glass of champagne as we toast to a grand future and a town in safe hands with me as your fearless and selfless mayor. I spare no expense for the people of Watterson, and as you can see –' she waves her hand towards a pyramid of expensive champagne bottles stacked up on the table '– nothing but the best for my voters. To me! I mean, to us!'

Everybody raises their glasses and cheers, taking a sip.

Pfffssttt!

A spray of champagne comes flying out of every adult's mouth – including the mayor's. The entire crowd is covered in a shower of liquid as they cough and spit all over the ground.

'Ugh! Disgusting!'

'That is NOT champagne!'

'What a cheap-skate!'

Zara and Sofia grin as they walk away, dropping two empty bottles of apple cider vinegar in the bin as they pass. Cookie low-fives them and they casually stroll off.

'Look!' says Zeke, holding the screen of his camera towards me. 'The replay looks particularly good in slow motion.' I watch the mayor's face distort as she takes her sip, followed by a slow-motion shower of champagne/vinegar spit from hundreds of people.

Mayor Lupphol stands there, stunned and drenched.

Claudio steps in and shuffles her off. 'Sorry, everybody, there seems to have been a mix-up here. We'll look into it. How about we just move on for now?'

Cookie, Zeke and I rush to keep up as the entourage moves away from the drinks tent.

Snatching a towel from one of her handlers, the mayor angrily wipes her face. 'What was that?' she whispers. 'It tasted like vinegar! I paid top-dollar for that champagne!'

Claudio whispers back. 'I don't know, I'll look into it. Just stay calm and let's get on with this. Big smiles, like nothing has happened.'

The mayor takes a deep breath and paints that now-familiar smile over her scowl. Just then, a boy with dark curly hair comes running up and grabs the mayor's hand. He has a cute yellow butterfly painted around his right eye.

'Mayor Lupphol! Come and get your face painted. C'mon,' he says, tugging on her hand.

She looks unsure, but Claudio ushers her to go with the boy. 'It will make a great photo,' he says.

The mayor hesitantly lets herself be dragged towards the face-painting stand. A crowd of young kids with freshly painted faces hover around. Spidermen, cats and mermaids all grin at the mayor proudly.

'Just something small,' she says nervously as she sits down in the seat.

'Of course,' says the face-painter. 'How about just a cat nose and whiskers?' She leans forward to whisper to the mayor. 'It will rub right off.' She passes the mayor a wet wipe.

The mayor looks at Claudio, who nods and gathers all the kids around. 'Make sure everyone gets in the photo.'

The lady starts to paint the mayor's face as the photographer clicks away. Claudio smiles. 'Oh, they're great shots. With all the kids gathered around, it's perfect!'

'Can I do the whiskers?' asks the boy. 'Please, Mayor Lupphol. Please!'

'Great idea!' Claudio says, before the mayor has time to answer. 'It will make the perfect kid-friendly shot.'

The face-painter moves aside and the kid sits down. He reaches around behind his back to the paint table, but instead of grabbing a brush, he puts his hand into his pocket and pulls out a permanent marker. Nobody seems to notice. In a moment of artistic flair, the boy draws a moustache rather than whiskers on the mayor – a French style one that curls up at both ends. 'Perfect!' he says, then jumps up from the chair and disappears.

The mayor poses for a few more photos with the kids and then moves off. 'Pass me those wipes,' she demands. 'I hate this stuff on my face.' She wipes her face and everything comes off . . . except the curly moustache.

'Um, let me just help you there,' says Claudio, trying to take the wipe off the mayor.

She snatches it away. 'I'm not a child, I can do it myself.' She wipes at her face again but the moustache remains. 'Is it all gone?' she says, glaring at him.

'Um, it's, well . . .'

The mayor whips out her phone and looks into the camera.

'*Aaaaarrrrrgghhhh!*' She rubs viciously at the moustache but it doesn't budge. 'Makeup! MAKEUP!' She yells. Out of nowhere, a makeup artist runs in and dabs at her face with powders and creams. When he steps away, the moustache is gone, but not before it's all caught on camera.

Now the mayor is fuming. 'Let's get the rest of this over and done with,' she says through gritted teeth. 'Fast!'

My cheeks are hurting from trying to keep a straight face. The mayor's getting frazzled, the cracks are starting to show and everything's going just as planned.

Claudio looks around nervously. 'How about the petting zoo? Some photos of you with baby animals would be great for your new campaign.'

The mayor huffs. 'I guess animals are better than children, at least,' she mumbles under her breath.

'What was that, Mayor Lupphol?' asks the TV presenter, shoving a microphone in her face.

'I said, the only thing I love more than children is animals!' The smile is back. 'Off to the petting zoo!'

We follow the mayor's entourage through the crowd and towards the petting zoo. I stay as close to the mayor as I can.

'You made sure there's no you-know-whats at the petting zoo, Claudio?' the mayor whispers to him.

He nods. 'Of course. We put a note for the supplier. I double-checked yesterday that they got our special instructions and it was all confirmed.'

'Good.'

The petting zoo is surrounded by kids waiting for their turn to go in. It's so packed we can't even see into the zoo. But the 'oohs' and 'aahs' from the kids tell us that there's lots of cute, fluffy things to pat.

Claudio pushes his way through the crowd. 'Excuse me, kids, let the mayor through. Thank you. Thank you.' He pushes open the gate and ushers the mayor inside. As soon as she steps in, she freezes. I watch as her face turns white and she clutches at Claudio.

'They're . . . they're . . . I . . . how . . .'

I squeeze between the crowd so I can get a look at the zoo. Instead of the usual baby goats and ducks and sheep, the entire petting zoo is FULL of guinea pigs. Kids squeal with delight as they chase the little furballs and scratch their fat tummies.

One kid runs up to the mayor and shoves a big fat orange guinea pig under her nose.

'Isn't he soooooooooo cute?' the kid squeals.

The mayor shrinks back in horror and begins to hyperventilate. 'Get. It. Away. From. Me.'

Three more kids run up to her, showing off their furry friends.

'Mine's called Flubber!'

'This one just did pee-pee on his friend.'

'Look at his little teeth!'

The guinea pigs wriggle around in front of Mayor Lupphol's face.

The mayor backs away from the kids, her mouth flapping open and closed like a fish gasping for air, holding her hands in front of her face.

'Don't step on her!' one of the kids yells.

The mayor looks down to see a guinea pig just behind her foot. She shrieks in horror and leaps in the air, landing on top of the TV reporter as they both fall to the ground. Guinea pigs scatter in all directions. Scrambling to get to her feet, the mayor grabs hold of a big bag of feed and accidentally tips it over, showering herself in lettuce leaves. All the guinea pigs turn back and make a beeline for the mayor.

'Aaaaaarrrggghhhh!' She screams as they clamber all over her, munching at the greenery.

It's hilarious. Like a scene from a zombie horror movie – except the zombies have been replaced by cute little guinea pigs.

Zeke's losing it. 'She does realise that guinea pigs are totally harmless, right?' he says between laughs.

'Says the guy with the completely irrational fear of the Coco Pops monkey?'

Zeke crosses his arms. 'Hey, that's not irrational! He's always staring at me while I eat my breakfast. It's freaky. Plus what kind of monkey eats cereal?'

Before I have time to answer, the mayor leaps to her feet and runs screaming out of the petting zoo. Claudio rushes out after her, assuring everybody . . .

'It's just a little allergy. You know, to the fur. She'll be fine. Everything is okay.'

He runs after the mayor, leaving the entourage behind. The TV reporter jumps to his feet. 'Did you get that, Amy?' The camera operator nods. 'Great,' says the reporter. 'Let's get a close-up.'

He brushes himself off and faces the camera, raising the microphone to his mouth. 'In what should have been a celebration for Mayor Lupphol, and an opportunity to connect with voters, the Watterson Fair has so far been a disaster. We will follow things closely today to see if Mayor Lupphol can make a comeback from the shambles.'

As we listen, Katie Lowe appears beside us. 'Well, that went even better than I expected.'

I give her a high five. 'How did you know she was scared of guinea pigs?'

Katie shrugs. 'I didn't. But there was a note in the booking that said to "be sure there are

ABSOLUTELY no guinea pigs" in the petting zoo. I just rang them up and told them the note was wrong and that it was supposed to be "ONLY guinea pigs in the petting zoo". I knew there had to be a reason, but I never would've thought . . . that! I mean, seriously, who's scared of guinea pigs?'

'Casey!' yells Cookie. 'The mayor's on her way to the baking contest.'

'We don't want to miss this!' I yell to the growing entourage. 'Everyone come on. The mayor's headed for the baked goods.'

With entourage, TV crew, photographers, kids and general spectators in tow, we run to the bake-off tent.

GREEN PEAS RULE 23

WATCH WHAT YOU EAT.
KNOW WHERE YOUR FOOD
COMES FROM.

The mayor has managed to pull herself together. There's no sign of the moustache, and the look of guinea pig-induced terror has reduced itself to a slight twitch just below her right eye.

Claudio stands beside her, whispering quietly. 'Breathe in. Breathe out. No children. No guinea pigs. Just baked goods. You don't have a baked-goods phobia, do you?'

She glares at him.

'Mayor Lupphol!' I recognise that voice. 'As head of the Secret Scrabble Society, it is my honour to welcome you to the great Watterson bake-off and thank you for agreeing to judge the winner.'

It's Grandpa!

'I have brought together some of my closest friends and we've baked you a whole lot of delicious treats. I oversaw the cooking myself, and can assure you that every one of us put our heart and soul and lots of other things into our cooking. And I present to you, the finalists!'

Grandpa waves his hand across the long table. Three dishes are lined up, and behind each stands a very proud-looking baker. Grandpa takes the mayor's arm and leads her to the first cake. A sweet lady with neat grey curls and a 'Vote Lupphol' badge pinned to her lavender blouse beams at the mayor. 'This is Edna Pritchard. She has been living in Watterson her whole life, is heavily involved in the community and is a keen gardener.'

The mayor shakes the lady's hand. 'Nice to meet you, Edna.'

'You too, Mayor Lupphol. I have voted for you twice now. Hopefully you will give my community veggie garden idea the go-ahead at the next meeting? It's been three years now.'

The mayor gives her practised smile. 'Well, you know, there are a lot of proposals out there and we can't go ahead with all of them. Now, what have you got here?'

Edna grins sweetly. 'These are my special Pritchard Scones. It's a family recipe passed down through generations.'

'Sounds lovely,' says the mayor. Edna passes her the plate and the mayor takes a scone.

Claudio ushers the photographer around. 'Make sure you get Edna in the photo with her badge.'

Turning to face the camera, the mayor bites into the scone. Straight away her face drops and she turns a little green. The cameras click. The mayor looks like she's going to spit it out but Claudio leans in and whispers, 'You're on camera. Swallow it!'

The mayor slowly chews, eyes wide, and then swallows the mouthful like it's a lump of dog poop going down her throat. 'What . . . was . . . that?' she asks Edna.

'Blue cheese and anchovy scones,' says Edna smiling. 'Do you like them?'

'I . . . I . . . they were . . .'

Edna's smile drops away. 'I would have done zucchini and spring onions. . . if I had a veggie garden!' She snatches the plate away from the mayor and removes her Vote Lupphol badge, crossing her arms over her chest.

Grandpa shuffles the mayor on to the next baker before she can back out.

'This here is Giuseppe Abini. He moved here from Italy seventy years ago and his family ran the local grocers for many years.'

The man at the table frowns, and his hundreds of wrinkles multiply to thousands. 'Until you turned our shop into a car park,' he says gruffly.

The mayor laughs nervously. 'All in the name of progress, right?' she says. 'Sometimes it has to be out with the old and in with the new.'

I look at all the oldies surrounding us and none of them look happy. Not a good choice of words considering the audience.

Giuseppe shoves his donuts towards the mayor. 'Here! Eat. You judge.'

The mayor slowly takes one from the plate and inspects it. 'Cream-filled donuts. Yum!' She bites enthusiastically into the donut. The insides ooze out as she gags.

'Not cream-filled,' Giuseppe laughs. 'Mayonnaise-filled. You like? It's new.' He bursts out laughing as the mayor spits the donut onto the floor.

'No spitting!' hisses Claudio. But the mayor can't swallow the mayonnaise donuts.

Grandpa, trying not to crack up, leads the mayor to his own dish. 'And this is mine,' he announces. 'It's a Singaporean favourite. You're going to love it. This is Ondeh Ondeh.'

The mayor peers at the little green balls covered in coconut. She looks at Claudio and shakes her head, but he nods towards the crowd. Everyone has their phones out, filming the mayor. The TV crew lean in. Grandpa pushes the bowl closer to her face as she shies away.

'Try it,' says Grandpa. 'It'll be good for you.'

The mayor's eyes widen as she takes a green ball from the bowl. She sniffs at it and looks to Claudio. 'Eat it!' he mouths. She sighs, closes her eyes and bites into the ball. Everybody holds their breath and . . .

Nothing.

The mayor opens her eyes. She chews a few times, nods and turns to Grandpa.

'Not bad,' she says. 'Not bad at all.' She pops the rest of the ball into her mouth and takes the blue ribbon. 'I think we have a winner!' she announces, pinning the first place prize to Grandpa's chest. Then she turns to Claudio and whispers, 'Now let's get out of here before I have to eat something else these old people made.'

They weave their way out through the crowd and I head over to Grandpa.

'I'm a bit disappointed, Ah Gong,' I say. 'You could have at least put some chilli in it or something. She looked like she actually enjoyed that.' I reach over to take a ball. 'You do make the best Ondeh Ondeh.'

Grandpa grabs my hand as I go to put the ball in my mouth.

'I wouldn't if I was you,' he says. 'Unless you want to spend the rest of the afternoon in the port-a-loo. She might enjoy it now, but she won't once the laxatives kick in.'

I look at the coconut-covered ball in my hand. 'You didn't!'

Grandpa winks at me. 'Let's just hope she hasn't tried to cut corners with the bathrooms at the fair.'

Before I even have time to process Grandpa's awesome prank, Tess shows up.

'Where have you been?' I ask.

She grins cheekily. 'Just taking care of some business.' She waves at us to follow her. 'Come and see how the mayor's fair is panning out. Not quite the success she was after.'

We walk out of the baking tent into . . . well, complete mayhem! Tess leads us through the angry crowd like a tour guide, pointing out one disaster after another.

'On our left here, we have the food vans and the results of the switcheroos you came up with!' She points to a group of people guzzling water out of a hose. 'This was where tomato sauce bottles were switched with hot chilli sauce. Here, the guacamole became wasabi – excellent suggestion by the way.

And here –' she points to a confused fairy floss maker taste testing his mixture '– is where a new salty fairy floss was created.'

A bunch of kids run past us as we head towards the fountain, screaming in delight and covered in bubbles. Tess smiles. 'Free cleaning for the kids of Watterson on our right,' as the Brennan Park fountain becomes the town's biggest bubble bath. All thanks to most of Year Three and a few bottles of shampoo.'

In the opposite direction runs a muddle of guinea pigs. Yep, that's what a group of guinea pigs is called. How cute is that?

The little furballs are all wearing miniature harnesses and are dragging a swarm of squealing kids holding the leads (they're not actually called a swarm, but that's definitely what they look like).

'Oh, and of course,' explains Tess. 'Thanks to Ethan Davey's dad, Happy Paws Pet Shop unwittingly provided some guinea pig harnesses so our furry friends could enjoy a little freedom outside the confines of the petting zoo. It only seemed fair that they should be part of the fun too.'

She points to a large crowd buying raffle tickets from a few kids. 'Over there we're selling raffle tickets to win a brand new red sports car with tinted windows, all proceeds going to the Watterson Children's Hospital.'

I stare in awe at the shiny new car. 'But how did you get a . . .' I stop. 'Is that the mayor's new car?' I ask.

Tess grins. 'You can thank Cookie for that one.'

Cookie shrugs. 'Just a simple change of delivery address. I'm sure the mayor won't mind. Her current car is only five years old, anyway. It's got a few good years left in it yet. And the money's going to SUCH a good cause.'

Things are going just as planned, and the mayor has some very unhappy customers on her hands . . . which is just perfect.

'C'mon,' says Zeke. 'The mayor's set to start her speech in ten minutes.'

Zeke, Cookie, Tess and I run to the main stage. The mayor's waiting in the wings, looking very frazzled. Her back's to us and she's talking to someone, her arms waving in the air. Claudio's in front of the stage fending off complaining guests. And the TV crew is filming EVERYTHING!

We sneak over to Claudio to listen in.

'I want my money back!' yells one lady. 'My husband has been stuck at the top of the Ferris wheel for TWO HOURS!'

'My hotdog was vegan! VEGAN! I don't even understand how that's possible.'

'When is the mayor going to reinflate the bouncing castle? My toddler has been jumping around on a pile of plastic for over an hour now.'

Claudio puts his hands up in the air. 'The mayor will make sure all of your concerns are addressed, and she apologises for any mishaps that might have occurred, but right now we're preparing for the mayor's presentation. Please be sure to stick around – you won't be disappointed with her exciting plans for Watterson.'

Claudio edges away from the growing crowd and we follow. He turns to Jess, the assistant with the clipboard. 'Well, this is not going well. Did you manage to find someone to introduce the mayor?'

'Sure did,' says the assistant, with a big smile. 'A real town icon, according to the lovely young girl I spoke to.'

'Great,' Claudio says, frantically shuffling through his papers. 'Can we get the mayor mic-ed up and cue her entrance music? Make sure the lapel mic is attached down low on her jacket – she hates it when it picks up her breathing.'

We make our way to the front of the stage. I want the best seats in the house for this.

'Does anyone know who's introducing the mayor?' I ask.

Tess grins, pointing to herself. 'I might know of a certain "lovely young girl" who suggested someone perfect.'

'Who?' I ask.

'You'll just have to wait and see.'

GREEN PEAS RULE 24

STAND UP. BE HEARD. DON'T BACK DOWN.

The Ants Pants are playing on stage. Mac's on guitar, Toby's singing and the twins are rocking out. They're actually really good. When they finish off their song, Claudio waves from the side of stage. The assistant runs on and passes a note to Toby, who reads it and announces into the microphone . . .

'Hey there, Watterson. Put your hands together for our special guest. A Watterson legend who needs no introduction, the heart of our small town and the person who puts some much needed Kooky into our lives . . . Kathy!'

Kathy runs on stage punching her fists in the air like a boxer. We all go crazy, cheering at the tops of our lungs.

'WOO, KATHY!'

'YAY! GO KATHY!'

Tess turns to me. 'Good choice?'

I give her a thumbs-up. 'The best!'

Kathy takes the microphone from Toby and steps towards the front of the stage.

'Welcome, citizens of Watterson, to a day filled with . . . well, let's just say unforgettable moments.'

A grumpy murmur spreads throughout the crowd.

'It gives me great pleasure to introduce the person responsible for ALL of today's events. She took over the running of our town eight years ago, and since then there have been a lot of changes. Yes, we lost the community centre, but we gained a lovely big car park that costs a remarkable amount of money to park in. I mean, I don't have a car, but with parking costs like that, I'll stick with pushing around my shopping trolley. Better for the environment too. And we know she's been trying for years to find money in the budget to fund the community garden, and we understand it's hard, but at least she found the money to refurbish her own office. And apparently get a new car too. Much needed things for our town, right?'

I take a look at the mayor on side stage. She's fuming! I could not love Kathy more right now if I tried.

'And we all felt the loss of the public library, but how else were we going to fit a second Burger Castle into Watterson? And as some of you might know, recently my beautiful Lego house built by the kids of Watterson Primary was torn down . . . with my best friend inside.'

The crowd falls quiet as Kathy wipes her eyes.

'And when I went to see the mayor about it, although I didn't get to speak directly to her, I was assured it was being looked into. And I'm sure you're looking, aren't you, Mayor Lupphol?'

Everybody in Watterson looks at the mayor, who stands frozen at the side of the stage. Kathy continues.

'Because we all know that the mayor wants what's best for this town. I mean, that's the mayor's job, isn't it? To have OUR best interests at heart. To protect us, and our town, and every creature in it – right down to the smallest ferret. So without further ado, I present to you, your mayor, as voted by you, Mayor Lupphol.'

A few slow claps echo over the crowd. I turn around. The entire town is behind me. Watching. And they don't look happy.

Claudio shouts from side stage. 'Play the entrance music!'

Mac counts in. 'One, two, three, four.'

But instead of 'Simply The Best', the band launches into a different song.

'What's this?' I ask Tess.

'"You Haven't Done Nothin'" by Stevie Wonder,' she explains. 'Toby and I talked about it and we thought it was a more fitting theme song for our mayor.'

Claudio screams from side of stage 'Wrong song! Wrong song!' But the band plays on.

Mayor Lupphol runs on stage and snatches the microphone from Kathy. She frantically swipes her finger across her neck telling the band to cut the music but they pretend not to notice. The crowd starts to laugh and cheer and sing along as the mayor gets more and more flustered. The sweat on her face causes her makeup to run, revealing the French moustache once again. Just when I think she's about to launch herself at the band, the music cuts out.

I crane my neck to see up into the AV booth.

There stands Fiona Gill – smug look on her face and an audio cord swinging from her hand. The mayor gives her a grateful nod and tries to compose herself. She pats her escaping hair back down into her bun, taps the microphone and turns to face the crowd.

'Hello, citizens of Watterson. I hope you've had a wonderful time at the Lupphol fair today.'

A grumble spreads through the crowd, but the mayor continues.

'Yes, there have been a few hiccups, but the most important thing is that we are all here, together, to support our wonderful town and carry it into the future. And with that in mind, I have prepared a video to show you the incredible things I have planned for our great town when I get voted as Watterson Mayor for a third term. Don't forget, voting is next month and I hope to see you all out in full force to get those ballot papers in.'

'Where's Zeke?' I whisper to Cookie.

She points towards the AV booth. 'Doing his ninja thing.'

Hidden down behind the equipment, Zeke has his laptop open and is running a cable towards the control panel.

The mayor gives Fiona the thumbs-up and she presses play on her own laptop. At the back of the stage, the giant screen flickers to life and a video starts playing. It looks exactly like the one we saw at the mall – flashy text and impressive animations showing our little town transforming into some kind of futuristic mecca. I see a quick flash on a split screen of Brennan Park being transformed into apartment buildings, but if I didn't know what I was looking for, there's no way I would've known what the plan was. It's like one of those TV ads where everything is cut together really fast with techno music and someone yelling at you to BUY BUY BUY and afterwards you can't even remember what they were selling.

'This is such a load of crud!' says Cookie. 'Do they really think *this* is informing the town of their plans? What a joke!'

'Yeah. But that's what we're here for,' I say. I sign 'GO!' to Zeke, who types into his laptop.

The mayor's video flickers once or twice and then disappears, replaced by the Green Peas logo spinning on the screen. Text appears below the logo.

THIS VIDEO HAS NO FANCY GRAPHICS
THIS VIDEO HAS NO ROCKIN' MUSIC
THIS VIDEO ISN'T TRYING TO SELL YOU SOMETHING
THIS VIDEO ISN'T TRYING TO HIDE ANYTHING
THIS VIDEO IS THE UNEDITED . . . TRUTH!

Silence falls over the crowd as a picture fades up from black on the screen showing Fiona Gill and the mayor in her office.

The scene plays out on the screen. Zeke even added subtitles so no one misses a thing. The town is shocked as they repeat lines straight from the mayor's mouth.

'The park won't be a problem.'

'I have enough "friends" on the council.'

'Line their pockets.'

But just as things start to heat up . . . BZZZT!

The screen cuts to black.

'Noooooooo!' I yell. 'Not again. Why does this keep happening?'

Cookie and I rush over to the barrier separating the stage from the audience. I scramble up it to see into the AV booth, where Fiona has Zeke's cable in one hand and Zeke in the other.

'That's enough!' she hisses at him. 'Who do you think you are? I'm not going to let a little brat like you get in the way of my plans!'

Zeke struggles in her grasp, snatching at the cable.

'Let him go!' I yell.

I turn to the crowd, scanning it for help, but the entire town is yelling about the video.

'What's going on?'.

'Who was that woman?'

'What plans for the park?'

I search for Grandpa, but can't find him anywhere in the sea of people.

'Let me go!' yells Zeke, swinging his arms and legs. Fiona just pulls him closer.

'You don't know who you're dealing with, kid. I know how to keep people quiet and make things just go away.'

Zeke cowers a little.

'We have to get up there and help him,' I say to Cookie.

'The only way in is via backstage,' she says. 'Unless you have some super-leaping power I'm not aware of.'

Cookie's right. The AV booth is up high on the stage and metres away, with a barricade in between.

'Move aside. Move! That's it! Make some room.'

I recognise Grandpa's voice straight away.

'Scoot aside, people. Vehicle coming through!'

The crowd parts as Grandpa moves towards the stage. Following slowly behind is a blue ute.

'What's going on?' I ask.

Cookie shrugs. 'He's *your* grandpa! Don't *you* know?'

We push our way back through the crowd as the ute stops in front of the stage. Dad steps out of the truck and faces the mayor, who's still standing frozen on stage.

'Dad? What are you doing?' I ask, very aware that EVERYONE is looking at us.

He gives me a squeeze and faces the stage. 'I have my own bone to pick with the mayor.'

Like a crowd watching a tennis match, everyone's heads snap towards Mayor Lupphol. She looks around in confusion. 'Do I know you?' she says.

'No. But you might recognise this guy.' Dad reaches into the ute and yanks someone out. The man stands next to Dad, shoulders slumped and looking like he's just been caught with his hand in the Tim Tam packet. He's kind of stocky, not very tall, and has dark hair and . . . massive Elvis Presley sideburns!

'It's you!' I yell, pointing an accusatory finger at him.

Dad smiles. 'As the mayor well knows, we've been having some illegal dumping issues around

Watto Mall recently. This is the man we caught on tape. Casey, meet Gus Jenkins – AKA Elvis Presley sideburns guy.'

'How did you find him?' I ask. I clearly underestimated my dad.

'You knew his name. I knew his car. Turns out there's not so many Guses in town with a blue ute.'

'Or sideburns that ridiculous!' I add.

Dad turns back to the mayor. 'Maybe if you treated your under-the-table-employees a bit better, they'd be smarter about where they dumped your messes.' He moves to the back of the ute and slides out the lock, letting the back flick down. 'Like this, for example.'

Like a rainbow waterfall, out pours piece after colourful piece of Lego.

'My house!' yells Kathy. The town gasps in unison.

'Tell them,' says Dad, shoving Gus forward.

He hangs his head and mumbles. 'Well, the mayor, see, she –'

'Speak up,' yells someone from the crowd.

'We can't hear you,' shouts another.

'Casey!' Toby yells from the stage. I look up and he snatches the mayor's microphone, tossing it to me. Catching it with surprising co-ordination, I hold it under Gus's chin.

'The mayor paid me to tear down Kathy's house in the middle of the night,' he says nervously. 'She paid me to do a lot of things to clear out the park. I got rid of the possums. Next was going to be poisoning the trees.' Gus looks up at the crowd. 'I'm sorry, I really am.'

'You should be!' shouts Kathy. 'Mr Piddles was in that house.'

Gus rubs his messy hair. 'I didn't mean to hurt anyone. Really.'

'I told you to get rid of that!' the mayor mumbles – but her lapel microphone picks it up clearly so the entire town can hear.

'Do you know how expensive Lego is?' says Gus. 'This was enough to keep my kids happy for the next ten Christmases.'

The crowd turns back to the mayor.

'We want to see what else you've been up to,' someone yells.

'Play the rest of the video!' shouts another.

The crowd begins to chant. 'Play the video! Play the video!'

Zeke struggles against Fiona's hold, but she won't let go. Kathy rushes at her from side of stage but Fiona sees her coming. She turns and, with her free hand, shoves Kathy to the ground. 'Stay back! All of you!' Fiona yells with wild eyes.

REEEEEOOOOWWWWW!

A wild screech comes from the Lego pile, and a streak of brown and white flies across the crowd. It leaps over the barrier, up onto stage and to the AV booth, launching itself at Fiona Gill's nose.

'Aaaarrrgghhhhh!' screams Fiona, throwing her hands in the air and releasing Zeke.

'Mr Piddles!' yells Kathy.

Fiona spins around with the ferret attached to her face, his sharp teeth clenched tightly on her pointy nose. 'Get this thing off me!'

The crowd starts to chuckle. And yep, I do too. As Fiona spins, Mr Piddles' body flies out, kind of like when you grab a little kid by the hands and give them an aeroplane. Mr Piddles sticks out horizontally from Fiona's face, giving her a sort of extended-ferret-nose.

'Make it let go!' she screams.

'Sorry,' says Kathy, laughing. 'Mr Piddles has a mind of his own. Bit of a rebel. Doesn't take orders well.'

Fiona swipes at the ferret frantically, but he doesn't let go.

'Help me! Help meeeeeeee!' she screams, running out of the booth. Zeke takes the opportunity and reconnects our video. Fiona and the mayor flick back up on the screen.

'Make sure this gets me the permissions I need,' says Fiona on the video as she holds out the wad of cash.

The mayor, still standing on stage, finally snaps out of her trance and runs towards Zeke. 'Stop that right now!'

But before she can get to him, Claudio steps in front of her, blocking her path. Glaring at her, he leans in and speaks slowly, his voice picked up by the mayor's lapel mic. 'You know what, Mayor Lupphol?' he says. 'I think I'd like to see what transpires here. I think the whole town would like to see.'

A huge cheer comes up from the crowd and the mayor shrinks back, forced to stand by and watch her own demise. ('Demise' is such a great word. Even better if you follow it with an evil laugh!)

The whole town of Watterson watches the screen as Mayor Lupphol takes the bribe from Fiona Gill.

'It's not what it looks like,' says the mayor, her lapel mic echoing her voice through the speakers.

But the town responds with a resounding 'BOOOOOOO!'

'They're just kids. Trouble-makers. They've edited it together to make it look worse than it is. She was just paying for some improvements being made to the town. Who are you going to believe? The mayor of Watterson, or some bratty kids who should be doing their homework instead of causing trouble?'

The crowd begins to murmur. The mayor straightens up.

'These are the same kids who have been disrupting the town with their silly pranks, and now they're getting hysterical over a simple business transaction.'

I look down at the microphone still in my hand. I roll it in my palm. It's time to be heard.

'Mayor Lupphol,' I say. My voice echoes through the speakers. It sounds so loud. Everyone turns to face me. It's just like the first meeting in the swimming pool change rooms – but times a thousand! I look around the sea of faces. I'm being stared at, which terrifies me, but there's something else . . . I'm being listened to. If I want to be heard, the time is now. I shove my nerves to the side and find my voice. Gripping the microphone tighter, I fix my sights on the mayor. 'Firstly, let me assure you that my homework is well taken care of. Wouldn't you agree, Dad?'

He smiles at me and nods proudly. 'Absolutely.'

'Secondly, no one is getting hysterical here. In fact, maybe that's the problem. Maybe Watterson has been sitting back too calmly for the last eight years and letting you run things as you please. That time is over. We may just be kids, we may not have a vote yet, we may not be able to "take you down", but what we can do is show people the truth. And if we show them the truth and they still vote for you, then we have a far bigger problem on our hands.' I nod to Zeke. 'Play it! And notice, there are NO edits.'

All attention turns to the screen as Zeke plays my favourite bit.

The mayor onscreen rolls the money around in her hand, looking at it like a dog would drool over a big chop.

'Don't worry about them. The people here are a bunch of sheep, blindly believing everything I tell them. Keep them focused on their own problems and they won't even notice the big picture. I'll tell them what they want to hear, throw them a big fair, and it's the only thing they'll remember at the voting booth.'

The mayor on stage cringes in front of the crowd.

'You know what, Mayor Lupphol,' I say into the microphone, my voice booming loud across the park. 'I hope you're right. I hope this is the only thing they remember when it comes to voting.'

The crowd grumbles as the mayor shrinks away, attempting to sneak off backstage. But as she reaches the curtains, they fling open. There stands Tess, hands on hips, doing her best impression of a superhero.

'And where do you think you're going?' she says to the mayor. 'I've brought a friend who wants to have a little chat with you.'

Senior Detective McKenzie steps through the curtain. 'How about you come down to the station with me, Mayor Lupphol?'

The mayor points to the screen. 'You can't use that. That footage was obtained illegally. You should arrest those kids.'

'Don't you worry about that,' he says. 'I'll have a chat with the kids later. But I'm not even talking about their video. We have the matter of illegal dumping to discuss. The footage from the Watterson Mall security cameras *is* legal and you have a few questions to answer.'

The police officer takes the mayor by the arm. 'It's probably better if you come voluntarily,' he suggests.

'But . . . I . . .' The mayor stops. An enormous growlish gurgle comes from her stomach, the lapel mic on her jacket echoing it across the park. I've never heard anything like that come from a human being before. It sounds like the mayor's swallowed a grizzly bear. She holds her stomach.

'Are you okay?' asks the police officer. 'We need to go to the station.'

Another rumble comes from her tummy. This time even louder. 'I'm going to have to stop off somewhere else first!' she says, bolting off-stage with Senior Detective McKenzie close behind.

Grandpa leans over my shoulder. 'I told you she'd be needing the bathroom,' he laughs. 'My Ondeh Ondeh are finally kicking in!'

The mayor bolts to the closest port-a-loo and slams the door behind her.

'Cookie!' I yell. 'Get a photo of that for the newspaper. I think it sums up the day perfectly.'

Cookie runs over and takes a snap of the police officer outside the port-a-loo, arms crossed, waiting to take the mayor to the station.

'I can see the headlines now,' laughs Grandpa. 'Mayor Port-a-Lupphol.'

Dad comes over and puts one hand on my shoulder, and the other on Grandpa's. 'I think our work here is done, Team Wu. How about we call it a day? Who wants some lunch?'

'Great idea,' says Grandpa. 'But not from here. Can't trust the food in this place.'

'How about The Funky Anchovy?' asks Dad.

'But Dad,' I say. 'You *never* let us go there!'

'Well, maybe it's time for things to change,' he says, giving me a squeeze. 'I've heard change can be a good thing.'

'Can my friends come too?'

'The more, the merrier.'

I round up Zeke, and Cookie, and Tess, and Toby, and their families – and Kathy, of course (with Mr Piddles) – and soon the ENTIRE tribe are crammed into The Funky Anchovy munching on Watterson's most delicious pizza.

GREEN PEAS RULE 25

ALWAYS TRY TO BE A BETTER PERSON. BUT IN THE END, BE THE BEST YOU CAN.

'You were awesome today, Dad.'

Dad sits on the edge of my bed and pulls my doona up around my chin. It's been ages since Dad's been home to tuck me in. It's pretty nice.

'Me?' he says. 'How about you? I didn't know you had that in you, Casey. You really stood up to that ratbag mayor. I was very proud of you.'

I shuffle down deeper into the covers. 'Dad?'

'Yeah?'

'Do you think Mum would have been proud of me?'

Dad gives me a sad smile. 'Shove over, Casey,' he says and I wiggle aside. He lies down next to me on the single bed and we both stare at the Mum-collage on my wall. 'I think you've got it all a bit wrong with your mum.'

'How do you mean?'

'Making her proud is not about being like her. It's about being the best YOU. She loved you for being you. Just like I do. She wouldn't want you to try to be like her. I don't want you to try to be like me. And NOBODY wants you to be like Grandpa.' He nudges me with his shoulder. 'Just be you. Stand up for the things you believe in, like you did today. Nothing will make us prouder than that. Okay?'

'Even if it means becoming a professional prankster?'

'Preferably not,' he says. 'But whatever you think is right.'

I laugh. 'Don't worry, Dad. I've been thinking maybe I want to become a writer. Investigating and reporting the truth to everyone, so people can make better decisions.'

'Or you could just be an accountant?'

'Daaaaaaad!'

He laughs. 'Like I said – whatever YOU want to be, baby.'

I smile and look at the photo of Mum on my wall. 'She was pretty amazing, wasn't she?' I say.

'She sure was,' says Dad. 'And that's something you two have in common.' He gets up from the bed and kisses my forehead. 'I love you, Casey.'

'Love you too, Dad.'

He walks over to the Mum-collage, kisses his fingers and presses them softly against the photo. 'Love you too, Trixie.' The corner of Mum's favourite quote has fallen off. Dad flicks it back up and pushes the blu-tack back against the wall. He reads the quote to himself.

'"The only thing necessary for the triumph of evil is for good men to do nothing." Smart man, that Edmund Burke.'

'Dad?'

'Yes?'

'Mum would be proud of you too, you know?'

He sighs. 'Would she?'

'Yes. You've been a really good dad.'

'Thanks, Casey, but maybe that's not enough. Have I been a good man?'

I don't quite know what he means, but I also don't think he's looking for an answer from me.

'Sleep tight,' he says, and pulls the door closed.

I lay there in the dark thinking about my mum. I think about how good it felt to stand up to Mayor Lupphol today and let everybody know the truth. I *am* like my mum. I may not have the same hair colour or the same eyes. Maybe I won't do all the amazing things she did in life – or maybe I'll do more.

I get up and walk over to the photos. I unpin one of me, Dad and Mum having a picnic in Brennan Park. It was taken just before Mum got sick. Dad's the only one looking at the camera. Mum and little baby me are both looking at Dad.

At that moment I realise something, something that I should have realised a long time ago. No matter what I look like, or who I grow up to be, Mum and I will always have something in common. We both love Dad more than anything in this world. And he loves us.

I pin the photo back up and pull out the 'Mum's thoughts on . . .' box. I turn it around and put a new white sticker on the other end. On it I write – 'Casey Wu's thoughts on . . .'

I pull out the first card and read it.

Trixie Wu's Thoughts On . . .

CASEY

You are the most beautiful thing I have ever laid my eyes on. Nothing hurts more than knowing I won't be there to see you grow into the person you are going to be. Know that you are loved. By your dad, by your grandpa and by me . . . always. Be you, Casey. Whoever that turns out to be.

xMum

I turn it over and take out a pen. On the back I write . . .

Casey Wu's Thoughts On . . .

CASEY

I don't know exactly who I am yet . . . and that's okay. I'm still learning. But I do know this: I will not be someone who stands by and lets bad people do bad things. I will stand up. And I will be heard.

Casey Wu

I slide the card back into the box then crawl into bed and go to sleep.

GREEN PEAS RULE 26

Lead the change.

A week later, I'm sitting on Mum's bench waiting for Zeke. Cookie's beside me with a new folder full of new plans.

'Mr Deery's totally on board with the idea of a school newspaper, so he's gonna talk to Mrs Keiren for us,' says Cookie.

We decided that we had made such great fake-reporters that maybe we'd give it a go for real. So Green Peas is now planning *The Green Leaf*, a school newspaper run by us. Cookie will take the photos and design the paper, I (and my growing team of reporters) will cover the local news and Zeke's working on a news report to accompany it for the internal school TV channel. This way we can keep all the kids (and their parents) up to date with what's REALLY going on in Watterson. Green Peas is also now an official organisation. Open and public. Less incognito (my new favourite word) and more out and proud, with solid plans for how to improve the way our school and our town runs. And we have more than fifty members! But not everyone has a t-shirt yet.

'Where's Zeke?' I ask. 'He's late for the meeting.'

Cookie shrugs. 'I dunno. He said he'd be here. Something about having our first front-page story?'

I cross my arms. 'Okay, but just so you know, I refuse to have the word "ninja" in our first headline.'

'Sorry I'm late.' Zeke rounds the corner with a large hessian bag full of something heavy slung over his shoulder like Santa Claus. He dumps the bag on the ground. It sounds like it's full of plastic bottle tops.

'What's that?' I ask.

'You know how we said that Green Peas are going to move away from the pranking and focus on some more practical ways to help? Things that are close to our hearts?'

'Yes,' I say, cautious of what ridiculous scheme Zeke might have come up with.

'Well, I thought we might like to start off with some upcycling.'

'Okay,' I say. 'But you do know that the recycling centre is on the other side of town?'

'Not recycling,' says Zeke with a grin. 'Upcycling.'

With that, a whole bunch of kids round the corner into Brennan Park, each carrying their own bag. Tess and Toby are there, along with a whole lot of our other schoolmates. They all line up next to Zeke and dump their bags at their feet.

'I don't get it,' I say.

Toby grins at me. 'I can think of a way we can reuse this!' He tips his bag upside down and out tumbles a heap of Lego. All the other kids empty their bags too until a giant pile of Lego sits in front of me.

'What do you say, Casey?' says Tess. 'Should Kathy get a new home?'

'100 per cent!' I say. 'Let's get to work.'

Toby rolls out a new plan for the house and everyone begins reconstructing Kathy's home. Zeke comes over to join me as I try to piece together a window frame. 'I just hope they don't knock it down again,' says Zeke.

'I don't think we need to worry about that,' I say, pointing over to where Dad and Grandpa are putting up signs near Mum's tree. Grandpa hammers a stake into the ground. The sign attached has Mum's favourite quote (with a slight update) . . .

THE ONLY THING NECESSARY FOR
THE TRIUMPH OF EVIL IS FOR GOOD
~~MEN~~ PEOPLE TO DO NOTHING.

Dad puts up another that reads . . .

VOTE HENRY WU FOR MAYOR.
BECAUSE HE LISTENS TO YOU!

Zeke's eyes widen. 'Your dad's running for mayor?!?!'

I nod proudly. 'Yep. And he's gonna win. So don't worry about Kathy's house – or our park. I know people in high places.'

I reach into my bag and pull out a present, tossing it to Zeke.

'What's this?' he asks.

'Open it and find out.'

Zeke tears open the paper and pulls out a t-shirt, holding it up.

'Cookie made it, but I chose what it says.'

Zeke grins at his new t-shirt. It's red with black writing saying, 'TRUST ME, I'M A NINJA'.

'I love it!' says Zeke.

'Yeah,' I laugh. 'I thought you might.' Zeke switches t-shirts and I return to my Lego.

Slowly, Kathy's new home starts to take shape. Cookie (of course) is great at Lego, so I just follow her instructions, snapping the colourful bricks together. It's seriously satisfying! I'm pretty absorbed in my work when I feel a tap on my shoulder.

'Is it true?' says Grandpa.

I put my bricks down and turn to face him. 'Is what true?'

'That you're hanging up your pranking shoes? Moving on to more responsible methods of affecting change? Your dad tells me your pranking days are over?' Grandpa gives me his best sad-eyes. 'I'm so disappointed.'

'Aw, Ah Gong, don't be sad,' I say. 'Just because I'm scaling down on the big pranks doesn't mean I won't still be sneaking fake dog poo under your bedsheets.'

'Promise?' He grins at me.

'Of course,' I say, patting his back. 'It's in my blood after all, right?'

'Right!' he says. 'Good stuff. Who wants some lunch?'

Every kid in the park puts up their hand.

'Okay, I'll go grab something. See you soon.'

'You bet,' I say, giving his back one last hefty pat.

As he walks away, all the kids laugh at the sign I've stuck on his back.

IF FOUND, PLEASE RETURN TO
WATTERSON POLICE STATION.

Cookie and Zeke look at me and I shrug. 'Once a prankster, always a prankster, right?'

THE END

DID YOU KNOW . . .

. . . that Nat has family members with otosclerosis, including her own dad and her grandma? Lots of the experiences and moments in *The Power of Positive Pranking* were informed by Nat's real life – even the story of Ah Gong's mum's teeth! The doctors really, truly did pull out all of Nat's grandma's teeth in the 1930s to try to cure her deafness. Unsurprisingly, it didn't work.

But as well as drawing on her own experiences, Nat had A LOT of help from the amazing Deaf community right here in Australia. It's a rich community with its own language, culture and history, full of fun and generous people. Nat would like to say a HUGE thank you for the help she received from incredible people like Asphyxia, Julia Allen and her interpreter Rebecca, The Royal Institute For Deaf and Blind Children, Robyn and Lise. And, of course, her very own PB.

In this book, Grandpa is an awesome lip reader, but lip reading is actually very hard to do. Lots of things can make it even harder – mumbling, speaking too loud, not looking at the person you're talking to, moustaches and beards. And not everyone who is deaf lip reads, so the Deaf community have their very own language called Auslan. It's a super cool language that uses hand movements, facial expressions and visual gestures. Nat is taking Auslan classes at The Deaf Society (check them out at deafsociety.org.au) and would like to thank her amazing teachers for helping her learn this beautiful language.

She also has to give a big thank you to Wendy and Endy for their insightful reads and support of the story.

DID YOU ALSO KNOW . . .

. . . the environment and climate change are BIG concerns for lots of kids, and sometimes it can feel really overwhelming. But there are lots of different ways you can help if you want to, and you can do things that work for you. Find YOUR superpower! Some of the resources that Casey uses in this book are real ones, which you can check out too . . .

treehugger.com
millenniumkids.com.au

ABOUT NAT AMOORE

Nat Amoore gets asked a lot of questions by the kids that read her books. Here are just some of them . . .

1. *What is your favourite animal? – Daisy*
   Ooooohhhhh, Daisy, there are so many! But I think my absolute, number one fave would have to be a tarsier. Have you seen one? They're so cute and weird and starey. Did you know that each of their eyes is heavier than their brain? How crazy is that? I once held a baby tarsier and almost passed out from cuteness overload.

2. *What was the best prank you have ever done? – Grace & Hannah*
Well, see, I'm not sure I can answer this one without getting myself in trouble. Let's just say I knew this girl once – let's call her Mat Anoore. At her school, when the teacher wanted the class to watch a video, they had to collect a TV remote from the AV guy. Mat would always take two remotes, secretly using one to randomly stop or fast forward or rewind the video. It almost sent her teachers bonkers trying to figure it out! That naughty Mat Anoore. I would NEVER do something like that.

3. *Did you ever fake a sickie? – Tene & Eve*
Funny you should ask this. You know the scene in this book where Casey makes the fake vomit? She uses the very same recipe I used when I was a kid. I REALLY hated cross country day. So, one cross country day I made up a nice fresh batch of fake vomit, added an incredible, Oscar-worthy performance (that sounded like blaaaaaahhhhh, bluururrrghhh, hruuumpphhhh) and managed

to escape cross country day. Unfortunately, I arrived at school the next day to learn cross country had been rained out the day before and so I had to do it anyway. Epic fail!

4. *Did you ever have a bad injury whilst in the circus? – Amelie*
   I sure did, Amelie! I once cracked my head on the trapeze bar while flipping through air and had to get a bunch of stitches in the back of my head. It really hurt, and it bled a lot, BUT I got quite a few days off work and watched lots of movies and ate heaps of two-minute noodles, so things could have been worse.

Do you have a question for Nat? Send her a message via her website at natamoore.com

READ ALL OF NAT'S BOOKS

THE WATTERSON PRIMARY BOOKS

'Nat Amoore is the next Andy Griffiths. Her books are madcap and wild, with an enormous heart.'
Kate Gordon, *Newcastle Herald*

Nat Amoore joins forces with acclaimed graphic novelist Mike Barry to bring you a story of four kids – and four superheroes – who are taking their future into their own hands.